SYDNEY SCENE

To the Blackstones and Hammonds, secrets are a part of life. But none as profound as the one that rocked Australia when the firstborn Blackstone, kidnapped three decades ago and assumed dead, was resurrected and assumed the throne of the Blackstone diamond empire. Rival family leader Matt Hammond was apparently none too pleased at the gala reception, and vowed revenge.

Mysterious stock trading and clandestine deals have led the Pitt Street moguls to declare Blackstone's ripe for takeover. All eyes are on Matt Hammond. New Zealand paparazzi have caught the Hammond billionaire wheeling and dealing—and romancing none other than his son's sweet-as-spun-sugar nanny, identified as Rachel Kincaid. Looks like the caregiver is giving Hammond more than some child-rearing advice in the back of that limo!

Despite whatever's going on in the Hammond household, those in the know are predicting a blowup to the decades-old feud between the Hammonds and the Blackstones. When it does combust, there's no telling who'll remain standing as the first family of fine jewels.

Dear Reader,

Much of the information gleaned for the continuity has come from professionals in many fields and I would be remiss if I didn't extend my personal thanks to the following people for their generosity and patience as I weeded through facts galore to find the information needed in the setup of the continuity. So, to Roy Cohen of the Diamond Certification Laboratory of Australia; Malcolm Jeffs, coordinator of the diving unit, Marine Area Command NSW Police; Kirsty Wright of the Crim Trac Agency in Canberra; Geoffrey Logan of the New Zealand Police; Andrew Burden of the Canberra Aviation Search and Rescue Centre and Iain Ballantyne of Air National Corporate/Skycare International, my grateful thanks for all your help.

So, too, I would like to thank our readers of the continuity for your loyalty in following our tale, and my fellow authors for the hours, days and months of work we have put into the creation and birth of DIAMONDS DOWN UNDER. Our relationship has been much like a marriage—from the heady excitement of gathering the six authors and developing the continuity idea, through to the ups and downs and roundabouts of working out individual story tracks and threading the scandals and revelations through each book without driving one another completely nuts ☺.

It has been an honor to bring the continuity, and the mysteries therein, to a close with Matt and Rachel's story.

With very best wishes,

Yvonne Lindsay

YVONNE LINDSAY

JEALOUSY & A JEWELLED PROPOSITION

Published by Silhouette Books
America's Publisher of Contemporary Romance

This book is dedicated to Gordon, Morgan and Tegan, for your patience, understanding and support through every stage of the continuity and beyond. Thank you. I love you guys so much.

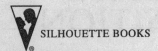 SILHOUETTE BOOKS

ISBN-13: 978-0-373-76873-8
ISBN-10:   0-373-76873-7

JEALOUSY & A JEWELLED PROPOSITION

Copyright © 2008 by Dolce Vita Trust

Books by Yvonne Lindsay

Silhouette Desire

The Boss's Christmas Seduction #1758
The CEO's Contract Bride #1776
The Tycoon's Hidden Heir #1788
Rosselini's Revenge Affair #1811
Tycoon's Valentine Vendetta #1854
Jealousy & a Jewelled Proposition #1873

*New Zealand Knights

YVONNE LINDSAY

New Zealand born to Dutch immigrant parents, Yvonne Lindsay became an avid romance reader at the age of thirteen. Now, married to her blind date and with two surprisingly amenable teenagers, she remains a firm believer in the power of romance. Yvonne feels privileged to be able to bring to her readers the stories of her heart. In her spare time, when not writing, she can be found with her nose firmly in a book, reliving the power of love in all walks of life. She can be contacted via her Web site, www.yvonnelindsay.com.

THE HAMMOND~BLACKSTONE FAMILY TREE

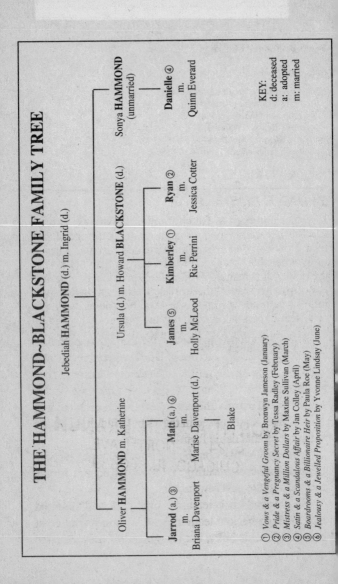

Jebediah HAMMOND (d.) m. Ingrid (d.)

Oliver HAMMOND m. Katherine

Ursula (d.) m. Howard BLACKSTONE (d.)

Sonya HAMMOND (unmarried)

Jarrod (a.) ③
m.
Briana Davenport

Matt (a.) ⑥
m.
Marise Davenport (d.)

Blake

Kimberley ①
m.
Ric Perrini

James ⑤
m.
Holly McLeod

Ryan ②
m.
Jessica Cotter

Danielle ④
m.
Quinn Everard

KEY:
d: deceased
a: adopted
m: married

① *Vows & a Vengeful Groom* by Bronwyn Jameson (January)
② *Pride & a Pregnancy Secret* by Tessa Radley (February)
③ *Mistress & a Million Dollars* by Maxine Sullivan (March)
④ *Satin & a Scandalous Affair* by Jan Colley (April)
⑤ *Boardrooms & a Billionaire Heir* by Paula Roe (May)
⑥ *Jealousy & a Jewelled Proposition* by Yvonne Lindsay (June)

One

He was alone.

Matt Hammond punched in the code that gave him access to the inner sanctum of House of Hammond and realised being alone was the one true constant in his life these days. Even Lionel Wong, the backbone of the business and usually the last to leave each evening, had gone home. Matt paused in the silence and drank in the satisfaction that came from being here.

It always felt like coming home. A feeling he'd come to look forward to during his all-too-frequent forays overseas in the past few months.

He dropped his briefcase on his desk and slumped into his high-backed leather chair. Weariness pulled at every cell in his body, but he refused to acknowledge it, or the hollow emptiness that dwelt in his chest. It'd been a helluva six months so far. Just when would life let up? He brushed the question aside. He had no time for the inanity of rhetoric right now. Each day brought its own challenge, and he would meet every one of them and win. Winning was just about all he had left.

He snatched up the collection of messages his secretary had left in the centre of his desk, a frown scoring two sharp lines between his eyebrows as the same name appeared again and again.

Jake Vance. Or, in his other persona, James Blackstone—the famous Blackstone missing heir finally returned to a glorious welcome home.

With a reflexive crunch of his fingers, Matt reduced the messages to trash and ignominiously launched them into the wastepaper basket.

He had no desire to speak with a Blackstone, whether he bore that name by choice or otherwise. The family was responsible for more misery than he cared to acknowledge. Traitors or thieves, every last one of them right down to Kimberley Blackstone. Perrini, now, he corrected himself. Hers had been the bitterest betrayal of all. He'd expected more of his cousin. She'd become his right hand in the business over the past ten years, but in the end she'd been just like her father. A Blackstone to the bone. And to think she'd believed the rivalry between the Hammonds and the Blackstones could be mended.

The slow rage that constantly burned deep within him fought to rise to the surface, but with his inimitable cool control he tamped it back down. There would be satisfaction. Everything the Blackstones had done—and the list was extensive—would come home to roost.

Matt leaned back in his seat and steepled his fingers under his chin. It wouldn't be long now and he'd be the one pulling Blackstone strings. A Hammond in control, as it should have been before Howard Blackstone stripped the family of its Australian assets with his unscrupulous methods. Blackstone had made his fortune by taking what he wanted, particularly from the Hammonds, but he'd dealt one hand too many when he'd taken Marise. Matt had sworn on the man's grave that he would pay and he would. Despite the glitch in his plans when Vincent Blackstone had refused to sell out his share holding to Matt back in February, there was nothing the Blackstones could do to stop him now. Matt's people had painstakingly approached minor shareholders with enough incentive that he was now very close to success.

He gave his desk another cursory glance. Still no message from Quinn Everard. He'd expected by now that the gem broker would have a solid lead on the last of the Blackstone Rose diamonds. Perhaps Everard's contacts weren't as efficient as he'd believed. That was the trouble with stolen property. It was difficult to find. Especially property that should have been a part of Matt's family's heritage and not tainted by the Blackstone name.

With a sigh, Matt leaned forward and popped open his briefcase to remove a contract from inside. A faint hint of a smile played around his lips. Success. With the agreement of the New Zealand Pacific Pearl distributors now in his hands he could fine-tune the launch of the Matt Hammond Heirloom Range of jewellery.

His own signature range.

He'd been working hard for months on developing the line of reproduction antique jewellery, and finally it would come to fruition. A man had to grab his pleasures where he could, Matt reminded himself, especially in a life like his that had seen precious few of them in some time.

Speaking of pleasures, this little foray into the office on his way home from the airport had cost him the pleasure of putting his son, Blake, to bed. Matt flicked a look at the Patek Philippe watch his father had presented to him on his twenty-first birthday and grimaced. Yeah, it was definitely far too late to catch Blake. But there was always the morning.

No matter how empty his marriage had become before Marise's departure to Australia, at least it had left him with his son. The void around his heart squeezed a little tighter. Had his dead wife had the last laugh on him after all? No, he didn't want to go down that route. He didn't want to even consider that Blake was not his own. As an adopted child himself he knew it shouldn't matter. Love and care and upbringing created the bonds between father and son, not just blood. But the question continued to prickle, like a fine metal filing wedged under the skin.

Was Howard Blackstone Blake's real father?

The thought made his gut clench. Marise had always been fascinated with the Blackstone family. But her death five months ago, as a result of the plane crash that had also taken the life of the Blackstone patriarch, had raised more questions than answers. Questions like what the hell was she doing with Howard Blackstone in the first place? Matt knew Blackstone would have relished rubbing his nose in an affair.

He wrestled once more with the anger that threatened to boil over. Howard Blackstone. It always came down to him. But no more. By the end of the month Matt's plans would reach their ultimate conclusion and he would exact his ultimate revenge.

He got up from his chair to file the new contract, dictated a short note to his secretary and headed off for home. Tomorrow was another day. He still had the night to get through and it would be long and lonely enough.

Subtle garden lighting spread pools of gold over the rain-washed driveway as Matt turned in through the iron gates that led to his family home in Auckland's exclusive Devonport. At least the paparazzi were no longer camped at his front gate. Five months ago he'd barely been able to move without having a camera or a microphone shoved in his face. Now the furore over Marise's and Howard Blackstone's deaths had all but died away, but the bitterness still lingered.

The formality of the gardens that lined the drive had once been his mother's pride and joy. Matt still questioned his parents' decision to move to a nearby assisted-living complex after his father's stroke. Goodness knew the house was large enough for them all and modification of a suite of rooms for his parents would've been simple enough. But they'd been insistent it was time he took over the property for his family.

Some family. A wife who'd been homesick and un-settled almost from the day of their marriage and who'd abandoned their vows and their child without so much as a backward glance. Matt could never forgive her for walking out on them the way she had—and especially not when she'd gone straight into the arms of Howard Blackstone.

The garage door slid open at a touch of a button and Matt pulled his Mercedes-Benz SLR McLaren into its bay, the rumble of its powerful engine fading as he turned the motor off. To one side still sat Marise's Porsche Cayenne. He really had to do something about getting rid of the Cayenne. Since she'd gone, he'd done little more than take it round the block once a month, preferring to use his other car—a Mercedes sedan—when taking Blake out. But like other less urgent things, dealing with the Porsche had to wait until he was ready. More important matters pressed on his time right now.

He'd told Rachel, Blake's temporary nanny, to use the thing. Marise had, after all, insisted on the vehicle for Blake's safety on the road, but Rachel had preferred to use her mother's smaller hatchback, arguing that in his child restraint Blake would be just as safe. She'd even gone onto the Land Transport Safety Authority Web site and printed the crash reports for her make and model of vehicle to prove her point. Eventually it'd been easier to give in to her demands.

But Matt knew from past experience, giving in to Rachel Kincaid's demands was a weakness that spelled trouble with a capital 'T'.

The interior of his home was softly lit, quietness all

pervading. He made his way along the passage towards the stairs with the intention of checking on Blake. He could have negotiated every room in the dark; there was no need for Rachel or her mother—his house-keeper, Mrs Kincaid—to have left lights on for him.

A small noise as he passed by the living room attracted his attention. His eyes alighted on a sleeping form spread out on the large couch. Rachel. Her rich nut-brown hair was pulled back in a plait, but tendrils had escaped to kiss the rim of her heart-shaped face. Like this, she looked about ten years younger than the twenty-eight he knew her to be. In fact she looked little different from the determined tomboy who had followed him and his brother, Jarrod, around as often as her mother had allowed it while they were growing up. Nothing like the suddenly sophisticated young woman he'd escorted to her high school graduation dance on the night that had seen her graduate to new levels of maturity beneath his touch. He'd betrayed her innocence, he reminded himself, forcing his wakening libido into submission, and he'd betrayed her trust. It wouldn't happen again.

She stirred again, as if aware of his scrutiny, then settled back into the plump cushions of the sofa. Her sweatshirt slid above the waistband of her jeans and slightly twisted across her ribs, showcasing the lush curves of her body. Her lips were soft and full, slightly parted as if awaiting some fairy-tale prince to come and wake her from her slumber. Matt clenched his jaw uncomfortably. What was he thinking?

Rachel Kincaid was his son's nanny, no more, no

less—and he was certainly no prince, fairy tale or otherwise. What happened in the past was a mistake best forgotten and filed back into the recesses of his memory. What he needed to do now was rouse her and send her home. Goodness knew what she was still doing here, anyway. Mrs Kincaid lived in her own quarters—a self-contained unit at the far end of the house—except for the times Matt travelled overseas. On those occasions she'd stay in one of the upstairs guest rooms so she could keep an ear out for Blake. It hadn't been necessary for Rachel to live in, and that was just the way he liked it. It was unsettling enough to have her in the house by day, but to have her live in? That would definitely stretch the bounds of sanity.

He reached forward to give her a little shake but hesitated with his hand in the air over her shoulder, the warmth of her body a tangible thing in the air between them. At her side Blake's even breathing could be faintly heard on the baby monitor. It suddenly occurred to Matt that Mrs Kincaid's quarters had been in total darkness when he'd pulled into the driveway. Strange.

Matt let his hand drop to Rachel's shoulder, his shadow crossing her face. She stirred and her eyelids flicked open. Her hazel eyes, initially unfocussed, sharpened suddenly as she realised he was there. Matt pulled his hand back, telling himself it was not regret that trickled through him because his touch had been so brief, but relief instead.

"You're home."

There was an accusatory note in her voice that set his hackles up instantly.

"So it would seem," he answered coolly.

"Blake was upset you weren't here at bedtime, like you promised," she persisted in the same tone of voice.

"My flight was later back than anticipated and I had to go into the office from the airport." Damn, he didn't answer to her, so why did he let her make him feel so darned guilty?

"Really? 'Had to,' Matt? On a Sunday night? You've been gone since the middle of last week." She pushed herself up from the couch and stood up to him, her five-and-a-half-foot frame no match for his six feet. "What was so much more important than spending time with your son? You forget, he's just a little boy—not even four years old. He needs his father."

"I forget nothing, Rachel." For a moment the air between them thickened, his words taking on a double entendre that related more to the spectre of the past that hovered broodingly between them than the present. Matt made a sweeping motion with his hand, as if to brush away the words he now wished unspoken. "Go on, head off. Start later tomorrow. I'll get your mum to see to Blake in the morning."

He reached for the baby monitor on the couch and switched it off. He had one in his master suite downstairs. Since Marise had departed for Australia at the beginning of December last year, he'd become attuned to the noises Blake made through the night. His fatherly instinct had sent him flying up the stairs to the boy's room at the slightest indication of distress before Blake could even wake properly.

"That's the problem. She can't."

Matt stilled. "What do you mean?"

"I left a message on your cell phone," she said with growing irritation, evidenced by the tension around her full lips. "Mum's been called away. Her sister, down in Wanganui, had a fall today. She's really shaken up. Mum flew down to help her."

The ramifications of Rachel's short speech hit home hard. No Mrs Kincaid? That meant…

"So I'll have to stay in house." She continued, oblivious to the silent clamour of denial in his head. "I can stay in Mum's apartment, or one of the rooms upstairs. I think upstairs would be best, given your erratic hours lately."

Matt fielded her pointed glare. "How long?"

"What?"

"How long is your mother going to be in Wanganui?"

"We don't know yet. Aunty Jane is quite a bit older than Mum, and rather frail. Hopefully we'll get a better idea in a few days."

"A few days." Matt repeated the words flatly. He could cope with a few days.

"Well, we'll know in a few days. It could be longer." She put up one hand to stifle a yawn. "Before I go, there's something else I need to talk to you about."

"Can't it wait?"

"Not this, no." She fidgeted slightly, pulling her bottle-green sweatshirt down over her hips and smoothing the fabric.

The movement drew his attention to the tiny span of her waist and the generous flare of her hips. She was dynamite in a tiny package, all right. A forbidden package, he reminded himself sternly. As forbidden now as she'd been the night of her high school graduation ball.

But that hadn't stopped you then, a cold, sly voice reminded him.

"What is it?" he snapped, irritated by his own inability to tamp down the curl of desire that snaked through his body at her mere presence.

"I'm worried about Blake." She hesitated, chewing slightly on her lower lip, clearly reluctant to continue.

"Worried? In what way exactly? Is he ill?" His hand clenched around the baby monitor; the plastic casing squeaked in protest.

"No, he's fine. He's over that cold from last week. Look, I really don't know how to put this any other way so I'll just come straight out with it. You have to make more of an effort to spend more time at home with him."

"I'm doing what I can," Matt ground out.

"It's not enough. He's become too attached to me of late. Surely you've noticed."

He had noticed, and it had hurt that when Blake had taken a tumble off his little bike on the back patio the other day, he'd run straight past Matt and into Rachel's comforting arms.

"It's only to be expected. He's lost his mother and I've had to be away a lot lately. He'll come right." They all would, in time.

"Matt, he's started to call me Mummy."

The words sank in with the weight of a sinking destroyer.

"He what? And you're letting him?"

"Of course not! I correct him all the time but he's

a stubborn tyke, you know that. He's just like you in that respect."

In that respect, yes, but in others? Blake's colouring was nothing like Matt's own sandy-blond hair and grey eyes. Blake's hair was dark, almost black, his eyes green. *He looks like a Blackstone.* Matt pushed the errant thought from his mind before it could take a stronger hold.

"It'll just be a phase he's going through," he managed to say.

"I think it's more than that. He needs some stability in his life. With Marise gone and you overseas so often, he's almost afraid to trust an adult. Next to Mum, who doesn't cover all his day-to-day care, I'm his only constant." She sighed. "Look, I know it's been hard on you, losing Marise and all the hideous media intrusion, but you have to think of Blake. He's your son. You have to be there for him."

Matt took a step back. She may have grown up here but she'd been gone for ten years. She had no idea how hard things had been and had no right to comment on them. And now she was his employee. A fact it would do to remind her of.

"Matt, I'm sorry, but you're going to have to do something. I can't stay here forever. You know when I took this job on it was supposed to be temporary—only through December until Marise returned from Australia. My agency in London is pressuring me to take up a new permanent assignment. With Blake being so attached to me the way he is right now, it will destroy him when I have to go."

Go? She couldn't leave. Not now. Not when he was juggling so many metaphorical balls right now. Aside from being on the verge of taking control of Blackstone Diamonds, he had the signature range launch coming up, and then there was the matter of tracking down the last of the missing Blackstone Rose diamonds. His plans weighed on his unstinting concentration. Concentration he couldn't afford to have broken by any further disruption to Blake's routine. As much as it tormented him to have her there—a constant reminder of the one time he'd overstepped the mark between chivalry and temptation—she had to stay.

Rachel watched as Matt absorbed her news. Short of battering him over the head with an encyclopaedia on paediatric psychiatry, she had no idea of how to get through to him. Blake needed his daddy now more than ever before, yet Matt remained so distant. It was crucifying to watch them and be helpless to do anything about it. When Blake had called her Mummy as she'd picked him up from his exclusive private preschool earlier that afternoon, she knew it was past time to swallow her fears and stand up to Matt Hammond. He'd been through the wringer these past few months with Marise's death and the subsequent media circus that still refused to end, but the man had to take responsibility for his little boy. Only he could provide the stability Blake so desperately craved.

"You can't go. I need you." His voice was hard, flat, as if he was holding on to his temper by a thread.

"We both know that's not true." She managed to keep her voice level, belying the tightly coiled tension in her body, even as his words scored a line across her heart. He couldn't even bear to be in the same room with her for five minutes longer than absolutely necessary. Matt Hammond and his unstinting sense of honour would go to hell and back before he needed her in the way she'd always dreamed of. She'd waited what felt like a lifetime to hear those words from him, but now that he'd actually given them voice they sounded painfully hollow. "If anything, having me here for Blake has made you distance yourself from him even more."

His eyebrows drew together ever so slightly at her words. She'd managed to score a definite hit. Ever since the night of her graduation dance he'd been totally and utterly aloof with her, hiding behind some cloak of misplaced honour. As if he'd taken advantage of her that night, instead of the other way around. In her youthful foolishness she'd thought their lovemaking would have brought them closer, not driven them eternally apart. That distance between them had made their current situation increasingly difficult, at a time when his son needed all the stability he could get.

"I have a business to run. I can't be home all day every day. Correct me if I'm wrong but you are a nanny, aren't you? That is why I hired you when Marise went to Australia." His grey eyes resembled cold, dark slate, the only visible indicator that she was getting under his skin.

"As a last resort only. Be honest with yourself, even if you can't be honest with me. If I hadn't been the only person you'd been able to get hold of at Christmas, you would never have hired me. I told you at the time it was a stopgap only. I have my own commitments in the UK that I need to meet."

Rachel shoved her hands in her jeans pockets to hide the trembling that would give away how upset she was. For Blake's sake, she couldn't afford to give an inch on this issue.

"Commitments? A boyfriend who's getting tired of waiting for you to come back perhaps?"

"Not that it's your business, but no."

"I'll double what I'm paying you to make up for the inconvenience. I need you to put your plans on hold, at least until your mother returns."

"Matt, you can't throw money at this problem and hope it will go away!" Rachel wanted to stamp her feet in frustration. "He needs *you.*"

"I know exactly what my son needs and I'll make sure he gets it. Do I have your agreement to stay on?"

He had her in a corner. She wouldn't leave in the lurch the beautiful child sleeping upstairs. Despite how she'd grown to love him in his own right, he was Matt Hammond's son, and for that reason alone she'd walk over broken glass to protect him.

"Yes. I'll stay. But I'm giving you fair notice. When Mum gets back from Wanganui I'll be returning to the UK."

He gave a sharp nod in acknowledgement. "If there's nothing else to discuss, I'll see you in the morning."

Rachel nodded and turned to leave, determined to put some distance between them before her anger and frustration found a new vent. His hand on her shoulder halted her in her tracks, the heat and strength of his fingers imprinting her skin beneath the thickness of her fleecy sweatshirt. Instantly her body leaped to life, her senses attuned to his touch, her heart craving more.

"Rachel?"

"What?"

"Thank you."

Her eyes were drawn to his sensuously full lower lip as he said the words. A faint shadow of dark-blond bristles marked his jawline, throwing his skin into relief and accentuating how pale and drawn his features were. It occurred to Rachel with renewed understanding how hard he must be fighting to keep his life together—both on a family level and on a business one. She knew only too well what he'd been struggling with.

Lost for words, she could only nod, and pulled from his grasp and his overwhelming presence before she did anything stupid. Like try to offer him comfort. To offer him herself.

Two

The next morning dawned with one of those impossibly clear blue sky days that you only get in winter. A vapour trail from a passing aircraft streaked a straight line of white across the azure background as Rachel loaded her car with a small suitcase packed with her limited winter wardrobe. Most of the summer clothing she'd brought with her to New Zealand she'd left behind in the wardrobe. After all, she'd only come to New Zealand at Christmas to spend a few weeks with her mother. She hadn't expected to stay on beyond the warm, sticky Auckland summer, nor had she expected to end up working for Matt Hammond.

When Matt had initially approached her and asked if she could help with Blake when Marise had gone to Melbourne to attend her dying mother, Rachel hadn't spared a thought. Her answer was an instant and irrevocable yes born of sympathy. As much as she'd never warmed to Marise, she couldn't refuse to help under such sad circumstances. But when Marise had continued to stay away after her mother's death, and her name had subsequently been linked in the press with Howard Blackstone's, Rachel's sympathy had been firmly quashed.

She couldn't understand why the woman chose to stay away from her husband and little boy at Christmas. Even if she had been having an affair with Howard Blackstone, as the media seemed intent on proving, how could she have rejected her son like that? Especially when he was old enough to understand the holiday and all it entailed.

Marise had never been right for Matt. From what Rachel had seen on her infrequent and brief visits home, she was nothing but a controlling and calculating woman who cared for little but lifestyle and money. Lots of it. There'd always been something inherently unsettled in Marise's nature, as if she wanted more, felt as if she was due more somehow. For the life of her, Rachel couldn't understand why Marise couldn't have tried to be happy with Matt. The Hammond wealth wasn't, quite possibly, on a par with the Blackstones', but it wasn't far off it.

And then, of course, there was Matt himself. Rachel felt the familiar tug of longing from deep within. Marise had been a fool, and she certainly hadn't deserved a man like Matt.

Rachel slammed shut the hatch of her mother's car

with a satisfying bang and climbed into the driver's seat. As she drove from the apartment complex in Takapuna towards the historic township of Devonport, she mulled over her discussion with Matt last night.

It hadn't exactly gone as planned. For a start, she hadn't expected to fall asleep while waiting for him, but then he'd been a lot later than she'd anticipated and her day with Blake had been trying on many levels. The boy had been overexcited at the prospect of his daddy coming home from yet another trip. When his bedtime had passed and there'd still been no sign of Matt, he'd thrown a tantrum of epic proportions, with behaviour quite unlike his usual bright and biddable nature. The gradual change in Blake over the past couple of months had begun to give Rachel cause for genuine concern, and she knew she was right to have brought her fears to Matt's attention. How he handled it was another matter.

The trip to Devonport was always a pleasure. Rachel had loved growing up in this bustling and interesting suburb. Her dad was a naval officer at the nearby base, and with his long periods away, her mum's job with the Hammonds had meant she'd spent a lot of time in their spacious and elegant family home nestled on the side of North Head, facing across the harbour towards Auckland city itself.

As she let herself into the house her ears were assaulted by Blake's excited squeal as he tore through the downstairs wearing nothing but a towel. He launched himself straight at Rachel, forcing her to drop her handbag and suitcase at her feet to catch him midair.

"Hey, you! Stop! Come back here."

Matt followed down the hallway, his longer legs eating up the distance before he came to an abrupt halt within a metre of her. Rachel clutched her giggling charge a little tighter, anything to hide the sudden flare of desire that swept through her body at Matt's appearance.

His dark-blond hair was in disarray, as if he'd just towelled himself dry, but that wasn't all that was in disarray. The towel he'd knotted at his waist had started to slip, exposing the hard, lean lines of his hip and the tapering 'V' of his groin. With a monumental effort Rachel dragged her eyes up towards his face, skimming ever so swiftly over his tanned, ridged abdomen and muscled chest.

Her heart skittered against her ribs. This man was nothing like the coldly formal businessman who'd arrived home so late last night. No, the guy standing before her was as different as a diamond from an emerald, and she wanted him just as much.

"Come here, you," Matt mock-growled, reaching for his son. "You have to shower before preschool. We made a deal, remember?"

Blake shrieked again and turned his face into the curve of Rachel's neck, his little body shivering with delight at the game.

"I'll get him ready if you like," she offered, doing her best to maintain eye contact with the man she'd willingly given her innocence to eleven years ago. The man who stood at dire risk of losing the only covering on his delectable body.

"I'll do it."

There was an edge to his voice that gave her no

recourse. Instead she stood there as his strong arms reached out and he plucked his giggling, wriggling son from her arms.

"You might like to—" Rachel started. Too late, the towel at Matt's hips slid away. She caught a glimpse of untanned flesh, a thatch of dark hair, before she tilted her gaze towards the ceiling. "Grab your towel," she finished lamely, her cheeks flaming hot.

Blake was in total paroxysms.

"You little stinker, look what you've done." Matt was clearly trying to hold back his own laughter.

In her peripheral vision Rachel saw him bend at the knee and scoop up the towel, before spinning around to go back the way he and Blake had come. It said a lot for his self-possession that he slung the towel across his shoulder, letting it drape down his back to almost cover his taut backside, instead of putting Blake down and re-affixing it to his waist.

The view of the ceiling was no contest against the long, strong muscles of his legs and his now semibare back as he marched down the hall. Rachel drank her fill of the vision, letting her eyes caress the length of his frame. A tug of longing struck deep inside. The whole exchange had taken little more than two minutes but it had left her shaking. Her fingers itched to trace those strong, lean muscles and intriguing indentations that made his masculine frame so incredibly beautiful.

She shook her head slightly to clear the mental image of doing just that. People like Matt Hammond didn't dally with the staff—he'd made that patently clear eleven years ago. Once had been a mistake. A mistake he had no intention of repeating.

She was his son's nanny. No more, no less.

As much as it hurt her to admit it, that would never change. And aside from what her length of stay was doing to Blake, it was also slowly killing her inside. You couldn't love a man for most of your life and not be affected when he refused to acknowledge you existed as a desirable woman.

Rachel collected her belongings and trudged upstairs, choosing the guest room closest to Blake's. She dropped her bags on the bed, deciding to unpack later, and went back down to the kitchen to put on a carafe of coffee, then started to make French toast, Blake's favourite. As she went through the motions, she realised she'd better start making some notes for her replacement as to Blake's likes and dislikes. For the most part he was easy to please and ate his vegetables with little coercion, but he had his favourite meals. With the first slices of bread sizzling in the pan she got Blake's backpack ready for preschool.

The phone rang just as she was putting the second batch into the pan.

"Hammond residence," she answered.

"This is Quinn Everard." The slightly accented male voice had a smooth, soft tone. "Could I speak to Matt Hammond?"

"I'm sorry, Mr Hammond can't come to the phone at present. Can I get him to call you back?"

Everard rattled off an Australian-based phone number before thanking her and hanging up with "Please get him to call me as soon as possible."

By the time she'd sprinkled cinnamon sugar over the French toast and put two servings onto plates in the oven, Matt and Blake had come through.

"Something smells great," Matt said.

"Yay, French toast!" Blake clambered onto the booster seat on his kitchen chair and waited expectantly for his plate.

Rachel slid the plate onto the place mat in front of him. "Be careful. It's hot," she admonished as the little boy snatched up the first slice in his little fingers. She took the second plate from the oven and laid it at the second place setting at the table.

"Here, this is for you," she said to Matt. "Take a seat and I'll get your coffee."

"You don't need to wait on me, Rachel. Blake's your charge. Not me."

"It's no bother. I was making breakfast for him anyway."

He accepted the cup of strong coffee complete with a splash of cream before replying. "And what about you? Where's your breakfast?"

"Oh, I'll get something later. After Blake's gone to preschool."

"Look, you've made far more than I can manage. What do you say, Blake? Should Rachel have breakfast with us?"

"Yeah, yeah, yeah!" Blake shouted excitedly. "Here!" He shoved a slice of bitten toast towards her, almost knocking over his glass of milk at the same time.

"Hold on, tiger. You finish what you have on your plate and I'll give her some of mine."

"Okay, you give Mummy some."

The air in the room thickened. Rachel shot Matt a worried look. How was he going to handle this? She saw him take a deep breath, the fine white cotton of his business shirt expanding slightly across the breadth of his chest.

Matt's cool grey eyes met her gaze steadily before he broke contact and looked directly at his son.

"Blake, you know Rachel is your nanny, not your mummy."

"But I want her to be my mummy." A tiny frown appeared between the little boy's dark brows and he set his lips in a mutinous line.

"Sweetheart, you already have a mummy." Rachel hunkered down beside Blake's chair. "We talk to her at bedtime, remember? And tell her about each day."

"But she's not here and I want a mummy that's here! I want you." Tears pooled in the lower lids of Blake's sharp green eyes, before one big, fat drop spilled over the edge and tracked down his chubby cheek.

"Son, you can't just have a mummy like that."

"Why not?" the tearful child demanded.

Rachel's heart ached at the expression on Matt's face. There was no easy answer. His next words twisted her heart even more.

"Because a mummy and a daddy have to love each other first."

"Don't you love Rachel, Daddy?"

Rachel caught her breath. She wished she could

disappear from the room. She didn't want to hear Matt's denial.

"We're friends, Blake. We've known each other a long time."

Rachel could tell Matt was hedging, trying to find the most diplomatic, yet firm, way out of the situation.

"But why don't you love her? I love her."

As if it could be as simple as that. It was time to step in. She didn't know if she was capable of standing up to hearing Matt's answer.

"C'mon, buddy, have you had enough to eat? Let's go and get your teeth brushed. We'll talk about this later, okay? I'll race you upstairs."

She helped Blake down from his booster seat, wiped off his sticky hands and face with a damp cloth and gave him a little tickle to distract him. Suddenly she remembered the call.

"Someone called for you, Matt, said his name was Quinn Everard. I've left the number on the pad by the phone. He wanted you to call him back straight away."

She heard the rapid scrape of Matt's wooden chair on the tiles behind her.

"Did he say what it was about?"

"No, just that he wanted you to call back as soon as you could."

"Okay, thanks."

It must have been important, Rachel realised, when she came back downstairs with Blake. There was an edge of excitement about Matt that hadn't been there before.

"After you've dropped Blake off at preschool, can

you pack a few things for me? I know it's not in your job description, but with your mother away—"

"You're going away again?" Her voice rose incredulously. "But you've just arrived home."

Hadn't he listened to a word she'd said last night? Had this morning's incident with Blake not shown him how important it was that he be there more for his son?

"This trip is unavoidable."

"So send someone else, someone from the office. Surely you don't need to go yourself."

"This is something I've been waiting for, for a long time. Everard believes he's tracked the owner of the fifth diamond."

Rachel's blood thrilled in her veins. The last of the infamous Blackstone Rose diamonds? She'd been here looking after Blake when Matt had received the news he'd inherited four incomparable pink diamonds in Marise's estate—diamonds that had been proven to be from the Blackstone Rose necklace, which had mysteriously gone missing thirty years ago. The necklace Matt's father, Oliver, had been accused of stealing. She knew how important it was to Matt to bring the stones back together and to show the world that his father was innocent of the slur on his name.

A sudden solution presented itself.

"Good, we'll come with you, then. Where are we going?"

Matt gave her a piercing look. "I beg your pardon?"

"I said, where are we going?"

"I'm going to Tahiti, but you're not coming with me."

Rachel braced her feet firmly and took a deep breath.

"Oh, yes we are. Blake needs to spend time with you. Your business will take, what? A few hours? It's a perfect opportunity for both of you, and it's away from here, from the memories. You're planning to be there what—two, three nights?"

"And then I'll be back."

"And you'll be gone again. Didn't this morning show you anything? Honestly, Matt, I just don't understand you. Don't you *want* to strengthen your bond with your own son?"

He took a step back, as if she'd given him a physical shove. His face paled slightly and the line of his jaw firmed. She knew, from past experience, he was weighing his words very carefully. Eventually he spoke.

"Rachel, this is a business trip. Not a holiday. You're not coming with me. Simple."

"Then you'll have to take Blake on your own, because I won't be here."

"What are you talking about?"

"I mean it, Matt. You have to put Blake first for once. If you don't take *us,* you'll be taking him by yourself because I'll be walking out that door and I will not come back. I'm not bound to you in any way, I'm not on contract and I'm tired of my life being on hold while you sort out yours. So what's it to be?"

As much as it would kill her to do so, Rachel had every intention of following through on her threat. Obviously something in the tone of her voice made him realise it, too. Finally he let go of an exasperated sigh.

"Fine. Have it your way. I'll have my secretary make

the arrangements and let you know when we're leaving."

"Good." Rachel scooped Blake up in her arms and danced him around the room. "Hey, Blake, we're going on a trip with Daddy, isn't that neat?"

The little boy laughed in her arms and started enumerating the toys he wanted to take with him. Over Blake's dark head her gaze met Matt's. She knew he was angry. Very angry. A tremor of an aftershock ran through her body. She'd never stood up to anyone like that before, least of all Matt Hammond. There was one thing he hated above everything else and that was to be manipulated, and she'd thoroughly manipulated him just now.

But it was worth it. Somehow she had to break through the invisible barrier he'd erected between himself and his son, and then maybe, just maybe, he could make room in his heart for another.

For someone like her. Someone who would stand by him, love him, no matter what.

Three

Rachel had worked for some very wealthy clients over the years but the speed with which the trip to Tahiti was organised gave her a new appreciation of the power of Hammond money. By the time Matt had arrived home that afternoon, a private charter jet had been organised for departure at nine the next morning.

Rather than be snarled up in rush-hour traffic, they covered the distance to Auckland Airport by helicopter, touching down outside the Skycare terminal, where the charter company's staff greeted them and introduced them to the customs and immigration officials assigned to process their flight.

Blake was beside himself with excitement and it took every ounce of Rachel's skill and patience to keep him occupied. Eventually, though, he settled into his plush leather seat on the Gulfstream jet and watched goggle-eyed through the window as the plane was pushed back in readiness for departure. Once they were at altitude, Rachel watched in some relief as, with the somnolent hum of the jet's engines, his eyelids started to drift closed. He'd been so excited the night before he'd hardly slept, ensuring, in his regular visits to Rachel's bedroom to see if it was time to get up yet, that she had little sleep also.

"You look tired," Matt commented as he unclipped his seat belt and stood. "Why don't you see if you can get some sleep, too?"

Just what every woman wanted to hear. Mind you, she did feel as though she was a bit of a wreck.

"I think I will. Blake's bound to be full of energy when we get there. I'll need a head start on him," she replied, her eyes skimming over him.

He'd surprised her this morning by coming through from his master suite dressed in his usual business wear. Not that there was anything wrong with the cut of his suit or the set of his tie, it was just that she'd expected him to dress down for the journey. Tahiti was, after all, a tropical holiday mecca. She hoped he'd loosen up once they were there. It would be no fun for Blake if Matt ended up involved in business matters for the duration of their stay.

"That'll be a good idea. By the way, Tahiti is twenty-two hours behind New Zealand time. We'll arrive about four-thirty in the afternoon, yesterday."

Rachel adjusted her watch to the new time zone.

"Right, I've got it. So are you planning to meet with the diamond's current owner straight away?"

"Yes. Everard teed up the meeting yesterday. I'll see you and Blake settled at the hotel then I'll call my contact. I expect to head straight out. I probably won't be back before Blake's dinner time."

"Will you be there to put him to bed?"

"To make certain, he can stay up a little later tonight. Given the time difference and the sleep he's having now, he'll probably be wired."

"I'm sure he will be," she said with a slight smile on her face. "But he'll be thrilled if you're there for him at bedtime." Rachel leaned over and smoothed a dark lock of hair from Blake's face, unaware of Matt's intense expression as he watched her do so.

"I have work to do. If you or Blake need anything, just signal the attendant."

The Gulfstream was spacious and comfortable and offered a full office set-up, which was one of the reasons Matt preferred this aircraft. He opened his briefcase and sorted through his papers, but his mind wouldn't focus on the work he needed to get through. Instead, his line of vision kept travelling down the cabin.

Rachel had reclined her seat, her eyes closed. One hand was tucked up against the chair back, her cheek resting on it. In his mind's eye he saw her reach out and touch Blake as he slept. It was foolish to envy his son that unconscious gesture but envy him he did. He shook his head ever so slightly. He'd been mad to let them come along with him. He would have been back at home by tomorrow night if everything went according to plan. But still, the prospect of a little rest and relaxation in the sunshine with Blake held no small amount of allure. As much as he hated to admit it, Rachel was right. He spent too little time with his son.

Matt forced his attention to the jewellery designs he'd spread out in front of him. He'd had personal input into each and every piece of the Matt Hammond Heirloom Range. A swell of pride grew from deep within him. The launch would see him realise a dream he'd held since he'd entered House of Hammond under his father's wing while in his late teens. Although House of Hammond specialised in antique and estate jewellery, he'd always dreamt of developing a range of his own— a blend of the past and the present with reproduction antique jewellery. His own personal and irrevocable stamp on the world.

It was no small personal pleasure to know that time had come. As had the time for a lot of things.

Growing up, Matt had always been aware of the undercurrent of jealousy that had tainted his father's life when faced with Howard Blackstone's success. The rift between the families had widened irrevocably when Howard had accused Oliver of stealing the Blackstone Rose necklace at the thirtieth birthday celebration of his wife, Oliver's sister, Ursula. Worse, Blackstone had even gone so far as to suggest that Oliver and his wife, Katherine, had had something to do with the kidnapping of James Blackstone, Howard and Ursula's first-born son.

As soon as Matt had been old enough to understand, he'd sworn he'd help his father clear his name and take

Blackstone down in the bargain. Well, he might have lost his chance to take down Howard Blackstone, but he would succeed at the next best thing. Taking control of Blackstone Diamonds.

Share by painstaking share he'd acquired power within the company. Now, with only a minor additional share holding, voting power would be his. For a moment Matt allowed the anticipation of success to wash over him, imagined the surprise and pleasure on his father's face when informed of the news. It had been hard graft, and risky, getting here. But it had been worth every cent.

And now he was only hours away from another success. The acquisition of the last of the missing Blackstone Rose diamonds.

The balance of the flight passed swiftly and it was only as they began their descent into Papeete that Rachel and Blake stirred. The flurry of disembarking, going through customs and transferring to a ferry flight to Moorea was accomplished in minimum time, one of the pleasures of charter jet travel. Matt wondered what was going through Rachel's mind as their limousine drove them to the resort where they were staying. Her sparkling hazel eyes were glued to their surroundings, drinking in the startlingly colourful array of flora around them. Blake chattered a mile a minute, gasping at the colour of the ocean, and he squirmed with excitement when Rachel promised him a swim once they were settled.

Would she wear a bikini? he wondered. A spasm tightened muscles deep in the pit of his stomach. It didn't matter whether she did. The creamy flesh she chose to expose was totally off-limits. He should be grateful that he wouldn't be there to witness their aquatic foray.

The resort they were booked into was beautifully set on a private lagoon on the northern shore. Matt had specified a garden bungalow, knowing his son's curiosity would literally lead him into deep water if they'd utilised the over-water bungalows available.

"This looks marvellous," Rachel commented as they entered the comfortably appointed bungalow. "Which bedroom shall we have, Blake?"

"Blake will bunk in with me," Matt said before his son could reply. "That is the point of this, isn't it?"

"Yes, of course. Lucky you, honey." She ruffled Blake's hair. "You get to sleep with Daddy."

Rachel's hand stilled before flying to her mouth to cover her lips. Her stricken eyes caught his. Matt watched as a flush of peach bloomed over Rachel's cheeks.

"I didn't mean—"

"Of course you didn't," he replied smoothly, but his voice contradicted the instant reaction of his body. The sudden hungry need that uncoiled inside.

"Could you get his swimsuit out? I'll take him to the lagoon while you're at your meeting."

"Sure, see you in five."

Rachel was standing out on the terrace when he finally brought Blake to her. The low afternoon sun promised a spectacular sunset, but its gilded kiss through the gauzy long shirt she wore over her bikini sent a fierce shaft of heat through Matt's body as he drank in the silhouette of her lushly feminine curves. Suddenly his business suit and tie were uncomfortably tight, less of the armour he'd subconsciously chosen for today and more an instrument of torture.

She turned to face them. "I was just admiring the sunset. It's early here, isn't it?"

"Between five and six, from what I understand. You guys had better make the most of the light that's left and I'll see you when I get back."

Rachel reached for Blake's hand. "See you later then. Say bye to Daddy, Blake."

Matt watched them stroll along the garden path towards the lagoon, feeling a twinge of envy at their carefree chatter. How long had it been since he'd allowed himself to simply feel pleasure? Damn, he couldn't even remember. But pleasure would be high on his agenda very, very soon. And it would start with the acquisition of the elusive pear-shaped diamond he needed to complete the Blackstone Rose set.

He went inside the bungalow and lifted the phone, quickly dialling in the local calling number Quinn Everard had given him.

"Mr Sullivan, please," he asked as the phone was answered at the other end. "This is Matt Hammond."

"One moment, sir."

After a short time another male voice came on the line.

"Mr Hammond, welcome to Tahiti. I trust your journey was a pleasant one."

"Thank you, yes. I'm calling to confirm our meeting tonight."

"Certainly, that is still in place. I understand that you have travelled here with your son and a companion. Please, bring them with you."

"My son's nanny." Matt corrected the other man's assumption. "It isn't necessary that they come with me. This is a business matter."

"Ah, but, Mr Hammond, we're inclined to be a little more informal in our business matters than perhaps you're used to. I will send a car for you at seven o'clock. And please, dress comfortably. I don't believe in standing on ceremony."

Because he would not jeopardise the successful outcome of the meeting, Matt had no other recourse but to accept. He threw off his jacket and ripped his tie undone, throwing them both on the bed Blake had chosen for him. Making tonight a social occasion didn't sit comfortably, but he would do what he had to do to achieve his goal. Acquiring the diamond was the only thing he needed to worry about.

He changed into chinos and a short-sleeved shirt and went in search of Blake and Rachel to tell them of the change in plans. He found them both splashing and laughing in the shallows of the lagoon. From the lengthening shadows cast by a stand of palms, he watched Rachel unabashedly frolic in the water. Her muslin blouse clung to her, moulding to her breasts and the curve of her hip, as Blake splashed water in her direction. Her hair was loose, and hanging in wet ringlets down her back. Blake squealed as she chased after him in the water, her longer legs making short work of the distance between them. As she bent to scoop the little boy up in her arms Matt caught a tantalising glimpse of bikini-clad backside.

Blood pooled low in his groin, a simmering heat that had nothing to do with the balmy evening air. He pushed his hands into his pockets and clenched them into fists. He shouldn't allow himself to be affected by her this way. The waters of his life were muddied enough without complicating things further by this uncontrolled reaction to a girl he should never have touched in the first place.

Girl? No. She was all woman now. The enticing teenager had matured into a beautiful woman. One who deserved to be made love to with painstaking intensity and focus. Not taken on the back seat of a car—her ball dress pushed up around her hips, her expensively coifed hair in total disarray—by a young man who should have known better. A man who should have refused what she'd so innocently, willingly, offered.

Any man who was not Matt Hammond.

He stalked out from the shadows. Rachel noticed his approach immediately.

"Hello. I thought you had a meeting."

"There's been a change in plan. We've all been invited up to Sullivan's house for dinner tonight. You and Blake will need to be ready by seven."

"No problem." She cast a glance at Blake, who was investigating something in the sand on the shoreline. "Is everything all right?"

No, it certainly wasn't. Not with her standing there as she was, her tempting body all but broadcasting in neon signs how available she was to him. As his eyes skimmed her form he noted how her stance stiffened, her nipples peaking into sharp points through the dual layers of muslin and Lycra.

"Matt?" she prompted softly, a note of entreaty in her voice.

"Fine. Everything's fine. I'll see you back at the bungalow."

He strode away with long, loping steps and castigated himself for every kind of fool for agreeing to bring her here with Blake. He should never have believed she would abandon Blake. Instead, he'd been so single-minded about acquiring the fifth Blackstone Rose diamond that he'd been prepared to agree to anything to make her stay on and had landed himself in an untenable situation at the same time.

When their limousine pulled up outside the traditionally designed home up in the hills, a casually attired tall, slender man moved out over the deep front porch. If this was Sullivan, Matt was surprised. This man couldn't have been more than a baby when the necklace was stolen; he looked to be no more than a few years younger than Matt's thirty-three. His stomach sank. Was this all going to turn into a wild-goose chase after all?

"Welcome to my home, Mr Hammond. I'm Temana Sullivan."

Matt took the other man's hand in a warm, strong grasp. "Pleased to meet you." Rachel and Blake climbed out behind him. "And this is my son, Blake, and his nanny, Rachel Kincaid."

"Ah," said Sullivan with a warm smile. "Welcome to Tahiti, Miss Kincaid. I trust you are having a lovely time so far?"

He offered his hand and when Rachel took it, lifted her hand to his lips, grazing her knuckles with an old-fashioned gallantry that sent a surge of protective instinct through Matt's veins.

"Miss Kincaid, your skin has the beautiful lustre of the famed Japanese white pearls. You will need to be careful in our climate. It would be a tragedy for you to bear any damage."

"Thank you, I'll be fine. We brought plenty of sun-block," she responded with diplomatic pragmatism.

To Matt's delight Rachel extracted her hand from Sullivan's grasp with a smile that didn't quite meet her hazel eyes, but he didn't like the way the other man's gaze lingered on her, or the charming smile he bestowed in her direction.

Their host gestured to the front entrance of the house.

"Come inside and we'll have a drink on the balcony before our meal."

They followed Sullivan inside. Matt was intrigued by his appearance. Of mixed heritage, his host had the darker colouring of the Tahitian people but his features were dominated by startling blue eyes and a shock of chestnut hair streaked with blond. Matt sensed an undercurrent of amusement from the other man—the sense that Sullivan knew his appearance had put him off stride.

"Please, take a seat." Sullivan gestured to a collec-tion of deep-cushioned hardwood-framed chairs positioned in a semicircle on the wide deck facing the ocean. A working pearl farm could be seen not too far away.

Matt lowered his frame into the chair and forced himself to keep a lid on his eagerness to cut straight to business. Clearly Sullivan wasn't in a mood to be hurried, and while it was frustrating being obliged to wait, Matt knew how to play the game.

Conversation remained general not only through pre-dinner drinks but the meal, served al fresco on the patio beside the subtly lit infinity pool, where Sullivan appeared to command most of Rachel's attention, explaining the pearl farming process in answer to her questions.

"So you're saying the colour of the host shell influences the colour and lustre of the pearl?" Rachel asked before taking a sip of her wine.

"Yes, and in the case of the black pearl there is only one variety of oyster in which it is grown, the *Pinctada margaritifera*. The pearls can vary in colour from pearly white to nearly black and many colours in between. Despite its name, they are never truly a complete black."

"The whole process sounds fascinating," Rachel enthused.

"Perhaps, if Matt is in agreement, you can all visit the farm the day after tomorrow? We have our expert over from Japan who will be grafting our next crop."

Sullivan flashed Rachel a smile that left Matt in no doubt that it wouldn't bother him in the slightest if Rachel had to make the visit on her own. It was definitely time to intercede.

"That would be fascinating. I'd like to talk to you

about a new range of jewellery that I'm working on and for which I'm looking specifically for baroque pearls. It would lend some real interest to the collection if we used a variety of black pearls rather than the traditional whites."

"If you gentlemen would like to continue your discussion I'd like to take Blake out to see the garden, if that's okay with you, Mr Sullivan?"

"Call me Temana, please, and certainly. Make yourself at home. When you come back inside, Philippe will show you to my study."

The men rose as Rachel stood and took Blake from the table. Matt waited in silence for his host to open the proceedings. It was a tool he'd found especially useful in business where people were altogether too eager to open their mouths. He wasn't disappointed.

"I imagine you would like to get to the point of tonight's visit. I have to say, I admire your patience and restraint. Another man might have tried to steer conversation but you've been satisfied to wait." Sullivan put his drink down on the table and leaned back in his chair.

"I'm not other men." Matt's answer was short, but within it lay a veiled warning. Don't underestimate me.

The other man smiled and nodded, acknowledging the unspoken message, then continued.

"I have something you want, something you're prepared to pay a considerable sum for. Am I right?"

Matt inclined his head.

"Something that by rights I shouldn't have."

"Correct again."

"And you are the legal owner of this item?"

"I have documentation to show so, yes."

"That won't be necessary. Quinn does his homework. His word is enough for me. Look, to be honest, I'm not entirely certain how my father came into possession of the stone. All I know is that it formed a part of a large collection of loose cut stones he'd amassed in his lifetime. As I said to Quinn, I will sell you the stone on one condition."

"That your family name remains out of any possible publicity about its recovery. Quinn told me. No problem."

Sullivan looked him square in the eye. Matt met his stare unwaveringly. Whatever the other man saw in his face must have satisfied him because he nodded.

"Quinn said you were a man of your word. I believe him. He doesn't do business with cheats or liars."

"You say you're not entirely certain about how your father came by the diamond. Does that mean you have some idea?" Matt probed.

"My father was Australian. He settled here in the late seventies, married a local girl and they established the pearl farm. He started collecting precious gems in the mid- to late eighties and I believe it was a short time after that, that he acquired the diamond, although I can't be certain of the date.

"He was meticulous about his records, which was why, when he passed away, I was surprised to find little documentation to authenticate the diamond. There was, however, a file with copies of his correspondence with someone in Melbourne at around that time. He only referred to his contact by their initials. B.D."

Barbara Davenport. Marise's mother. So they'd been right after all. She *had* been the missing link. Matt couldn't wait to tell Jarrod, his brother, the news. It explained why the original four diamonds had come to be in Marise's possession at the time of her death. Obviously Barbara had only ever sold the one stone. Had she kept the others as a nest egg, he wondered, or had the sale of the first stone been so difficult she'd elected to hold on to the others? Whatever her reasons, they'd never know the full truth behind them.

"May I see the stone?" He kept his voice low and steady, yet inside his chest his heart hammered in excitement.

"Certainly, come with me."

The room they entered was a type of study-cum-workroom lined with glass display cases of pearls in varying colour, shape and texture. Matt watched his host open a wall safe and remove a single black velvet case.

His chest tightened as Sullivan put the case down on a matching velvet cloth on the work desk and turned it to face Matt.

"Here, tell me if it's what you're looking for."

He flipped up the lid on the case. Matt's breath momentarily shuddered to a halt in his lungs at the sight of the pear-shaped pink diamond as it sparkled against its white satin bed. He reached blindly into his pocket, extracted his loupe and fitted it to his eye. He reached out with tingling fingers to lift the stone from its resting place, drinking in the flash of pink fire that blazed from the stone's core.

Mentally he ran through the checklist as he held the stone closer for inspection. Fancy Intense Pink, pear cut, virtually internally flawless, weight approximately ten carats. The match in colour and clarity to the other four seven-carat stones he'd inherited on Marise's death was undeniable, even without more specialised investigation. Deep in his gut he knew this was the one.

Carefully he placed the stone back on its cushion.

"It's what I'm looking for."

"I'm glad. For whatever reason my father acquired the stone, it doesn't do us any good to be associated with stolen property."

Sullivan closed the lid on the velvet case, and Matt felt a pang of loss as he put the stone back into the wall safe and swung the dial to reset the lock.

"Now we know I have what you want, let's get down to business."

Four

Matt stretched out on the sun lounger and soaked up the glorious heated rays of the sun. He couldn't remember the last time he'd relaxed like this. The sensation had become alien to him, yet at the same time remained as familiar as a long-lost habit.

His mind skimmed over the success of yesterday's meeting. Not only had he and Sullivan come to an arrangement about the diamond, which he would collect as soon as the confirmation of funds transfer came through, but they'd discussed a mutually lucrative arrangement regarding the black baroque pearls which would take the Matt Hammond Heirloom Range to even greater heights.

Now there was only one fly in the ointment. Rachel.

His hearing became attuned to the gentle sound of her breathing, his senses on full alert and prickling with awareness at her close proximity on the lounger next to him. Blake had begged at breakfast to participate in the junior guests' treasure hunt and sand castle competition on the beach. After checking into the details, Matt had left Blake in the care of the children's group supervisors. Right now he knew he'd made a terrible mistake. Without the buffer of his son there was nothing to dilute Rachel's presence. Or his reaction to it.

She was wearing a turquoise bikini, the one she'd barely managed to hide yesterday. On its own it was quite innocent, cut neither too low nor too high. On any other woman Matt knew it wouldn't have bothered him in the least, nor attracted his attention. Yet he could barely keep his gaze to himself. Damn. He shifted again on the lounger as his body stirred and he became increasingly uncomfortable.

She was torment in a compact package. In his peripheral vision he could see the light sprinkling of freckles on her shoulders, their pattern trailing down her chest and into the valley between the gentle swell of her breasts. An image of him slowly, painstakingly, tracing his tongue, from one pigmented patch to the next, burned onto his retinas sending a fireball of need deep down to his groin. Damn, this had to stop.

"I'm going for a swim," he announced suddenly, and pushed up off the lounger before Rachel could respond.

He dove from the edge of the pool, determined that distance from temptation would be his rescue, but the water's temperature did little to soothe the ache of desire that simmered through his veins. The silky glide of the swimming pool water across his almost-naked body only heightened the growing want inside him. With the volume of holiday makers in the pool, swimming one punishing lap after the other was impossible. Surcease, it seemed, was equally so.

Distraction, that's what he needed. He slowed his pace and changed to a slow breast stroke, using the opportunity to scan the occupants at the pool's sunken bar. Yes, a perfect opportunity presented itself with a slender blonde seated in the water. One way or another he'd scour Rachel from his thoughts.

An hour of distinctly unscintillating conversation later he returned to the bungalow. Rachel had long since left the poolside and there was still another hour to go before he needed to collect Blake from down at the beach. He'd taken a stroll past the activities on his way back and the sight of his little boy industriously and happily engaged had been a welcome one.

As he stepped inside the main lounge of the bungalow he heard a small cry of pain from Rachel's room. Concern overrode any desire to preserve her privacy and he covered the distance to her door quickly.

"What is it? Are you all right?" he asked as he opened the door.

Rachel spun around at the intrusion. Dressed in her bra and panties, she wore no less than she had poolside, yet here, in the intimacy of her bedroom she felt infinitely more vulnerable. Quickly she reached for her sundress, holding it to her like some outraged maiden determined to preserve her dignity. Her body, though, instantly reacted in contradiction to her action. Her nipples tightened in response to his presence, and her breasts grew full and heavy, aching for his touch.

"It's nothing," she answered a little unsteadily. "I just caught a bit too much sun today, that's all. I was trying to put some aloe gel on but I can't reach all of my back."

"Give it to me." Matt came closer and took the tube from her suddenly nerveless fingers. "I thought you used sunblock."

"I did, but it's been a while since I've just lain about like that doing nothing. Really, it's all right. I'll stay covered up from now on. You don't have to— Oh!"

The sensation of his fingers, slicked with gel, across the back of her shoulders and down her spine sent a shiver through her body that had nothing to do with the temperature of the gel and everything to do with his divinely gentle touch. The soft pressure of his strong fingers sent electric tingles up and down her back with each sweep of his hand.

As he stroked across the small of her back, her womb contracted tightly and she fought to hold back a moan. This felt so good. *He* felt so good. Her intensely heat-sensitive skin felt the warmth that emanated from him as he stood at her back.

"I'm going to undo your bra strap," he said in a voice that sounded surprisingly unaffected. "There's no point in missing anywhere. You don't want to peel."

"Of…of course," Rachel stammered, clutching at the cups of her bra as the shoulder straps threatened to slide down her arms.

"You have a line from the strap of your bikini."

"I suppose I'm burnt on either side?" She fought to keep the tone of her voice level, but inside she was a tangled mess.

"Pink, but not too bad."

Her breath caught in her throat as he traced one finger along the upper and lower line of her strap mark, inadvertently touching the side of her breast as he did so. Suddenly his hand dropped away.

"I'm sorry, Rachel, I didn't mean—"

She whirled around. "No, it's okay. Thank you, the sunburn feels much better now."

He was so close she could feel his breath on her skin, see the tiny silver striations in the irises of his cool grey eyes. It would be so easy to let her dress slide away, to lift her arms to his shoulders, slide her hands around his neck and lift herself up to kiss him.

She watched as his pupils dilated, heard his breathing become uneven.

"Matt?"

The soft slither of cotton, swiftly followed by the scratchier lace of her bra, across the front of her body was the last conscious sensation she was aware of before she followed through on her instincts. Beneath her hands the strong muscles of his shoulders flexed as she skimmed her fingers across their breadth, linking them behind his neck. She went up on tiptoe, offering her mouth to him, offering herself, maintaining eye contact as if she could will him to surrender to his feelings.

She drew her body in alignment with his, a groan of

pure pleasure rippling from her throat as her aching breasts pressed against the hard muscles of his chest, as the soft curve of her belly pressed against his. There was no mistaking the hard ridge of arousal in his swim trunks, nor the scorching heat that shimmered in waves off his skin.

With an answering growl he bent his head, pressing his lips to hers in a hard possession that took her breath away and replaced it with a clawing need that had remained unanswered for eleven long years. She pressed closer into him, shuddering in delight as his arm swept around her waist, drawing her hard against the lean strength of his body.

She drove her hands up into his hair, clutching him more tightly to her as her hips ground against his erection. She wanted him more than she'd ever wanted anything in her life. Her body remembered his touch, his inexplicable scent, and it excited her even more to feel him and know that she wrought this reaction from him.

His tongue slid past her lips to meet and duel with hers. Even the taste of him was addictive. She suckled his tongue, drawing him deeper into her mouth the way she craved to draw him deep within her body. A throb of pure lust pulsed within her, sending sensation spiralling through her body, weakening her knees. She buckled, falling back onto the bed, drawing Matt with her, over her.

She reached for him again, her hands running across his chest, tracing the outline of his nipples, a small smile playing across her lips as she felt them retract and tighten at her touch. She caught his top lip between hers and softly, gently, traced the tip of her tongue along the moist heat of his skin. When he groaned again, she repeated the action, this time taking in his bottom lip, relishing the tremor that ran through his body at her touch.

Her hands glided down his torso. Lord, he was magnificent. His strength and muscle were overlaid by the goose bumps that rose on his flesh as she outlined his ribs, then dipped one hand lower to his belly. She travelled lower still to the 'V' of his groin that had so enticed her only two days ago.

She slid past the still-damp constriction of the waist band of his swim trunks to find the hard silken length of him. At the light brush of her fingertips she felt his arousal buck against her palm, and she closed her fist around his shaft, sheathing him with a gentle stroke.

His body stiffened at her touch, as if he was about to pull away, but she strengthened the stroke of her hand, drawing to the tip before sliding like a hot cuff to his base again.

Rachel caught his lower lip between her teeth and sucked against it in a rhythmic motion that mirrored the movement of her hands, increasing in pressure and speed until she lost all track of intent and could focus only on the sensations that wound tighter and tighter still deep within her core.

His body began to tremble at her assault and he pressed against her hand, his hips straining as if to amplify her actions. She felt him grow even harder, his tip swelling, then suddenly he thrust hard against her hand, a raw groan ripping from his throat.

"No!"

Matt broke free and staggered to his feet. His body screamed in denial, begging the release her touch promised. This was wrong. It was all wrong. She was Rachel, his son's nanny, his housekeeper's daughter! He'd taken advantage of her trust once before, when she'd been just shy of eighteen and he twenty-three—a young *man* who should have known better. He would not do it again.

"What is it? What's wrong?" Rachel's voice intruded on the fog that encapsulated his mind.

"You can ask that?" he growled.

He flung an angry scowl at her and forced himself to ignore the flush of desire across her sun-tinted skin and the pointed tips of her nipples, which begged for his touch. He clenched his hands into fists to halt his instinct to reach out and gather her silky curves against his now bereft body.

"Matt, please. Don't fight this thing between us. At least let us have this."

His eyes locked on her lips. Lips that were swollen with their kisses, lips that begged to be kissed again.

"No. This was a mistake. I should never have touched you."

He spun and turned away. He needed distance—right now.

"But I touched you. I wanted to do it, Matt. You wanted it too. How can you say it's a mistake? We're consenting adults. There's no reason why we can't—"

"No reason? For me there's every reason. Aside from the fact that as your employer I'm accountable for you, I have no desire to be caught up in another scandal—

let alone another relationship. Can you imagine what the press would do if they found out we'd been intimate after your high school dance and that you were now working for me? Under my roof every night? You'd be roasted in the media. Give me some credit for taking responsibility for what's mine to protect."

"I'm not asking for your protection, dammit! Matt, I lo—"

"Don't. Don't say it."

Rachel went up onto her knees, totally unashamed of her near nakedness. "So you're running away again?"

"I don't run, Rachel. I create distance when it's necessary."

"Matt, get real. When it comes to running away you're an emotional marathon champion. It's okay to face the truth. We've always been like this together. What happened eleven years ago was going to happen sooner or later. And it will always be there between us. It's not a crime to give in to that attraction."

"It is for me."

As her bedroom door slammed shut behind him, Rachel sank back on her heels. Her mind reeled with his rejection, yet her body still screamed for his touch. Slowly she got up from the bed gathered her sundress and bra from the floor and redressed. Somehow, someday, she'd get through to him. He'd responded like a flare to her touch. As much as he tried to deny it, his attraction for her equalled hers for him. That much between them, at least, had never changed.

When she came through to the lounge Matt was dressed in shorts and a polo shirt and stood at the door, looking out across the gardens. As she approached him he turned to face her, his face an inscrutable mask. Even though he was dressed casually there was something about the set of his shoulders and the expression in his grey eyes that told her his defences were up in full force. She supposed she should take some consolation in that he thought he needed to armour himself against her.

"I've contacted our pilot. We leave in the morning."

"So soon?" Shock poured through her with the efficiency of iced water. "But what about the diamond?"

"If my transactions with Sullivan aren't complete by morning I'll arrange for the stone to be safe-handed directly to Danielle Hammond in Australia."

"And the trip to the pearl farm? We're expected there tomorrow."

"So eager to see Temana Sullivan again, Rachel? Don't tell me you're planning on using him as a backstop because I said no."

Rachel saw red. How dare he tar her with the same brush as his ex-wife? But she drew short of bringing Marise's name into the mix. "Don't judge me by other people's standards. I was thinking nothing of the sort. You're overreacting."

"Overreacting? I don't think so. As you'll remember, this was supposed to be a business trip, not pleasure. If you want to see Sullivan again you can do it on your own time."

"For the last time, I'm not interested in him." *It's only ever been you,* she wanted to scream but knew it would be useless. "What about Blake? He's having such a wonderful time. This was a perfect opportunity for the two of you to spend more time together."

"Blake's young. He'll cope."

And you say you're not running away? The words remained locked in her throat. As much as he denied it, Matt was running away again—from her. And worse, with her actions she'd destroyed the precious little time he'd been enjoying with Blake. Sadly, there was nothing she could do now but accede to his instructions.

"I'll start packing his things. What time do we have to be ready?"

"By ten, and don't worry about his things. I'll take care of them."

If he'd slapped her with a chilled wet flannel, his rejection couldn't have been more complete. Cold fingers of failure, tinged with regret, tightened like a fist around her heart. He was so closed up emotionally, driven by those damned diamonds and what Howard Blackstone had done to him and his family, that there was room for nothing and no one else in his heart. The knowledge that she'd been instrumental in effectively sealing up that window to his heart was a heavy mantle to bear.

Five

As their jet lifted off from Papeete's airport at midday the next day, Matt let his head fall back against his chair in relief. By later this evening they'd be back home in Devonport, and life as he had come to know it would resume. The past twenty-four hours had been absolute torment. He was used to denial; he'd lived with it for longer than he cared to remember. But the systematic breakdown of his marriage with Marise prior to her jaunt to Australia was not on a par with the craving for Rachel that shredded his very soul.

He could barely look at her without reliving the feel of her touch on his body. He hardened in response to the memory. Yesterday had been categorical proof he should have trusted his instincts and stayed well away. Even after all this time, she remained his one great weakness, and weakness couldn't be tolerated. Under any circumstance.

It would have been all too easy to lose himself in the comfort of her body. To forget the infidelity of his wife, the failure of his marriage, as well as his own failures as a husband and father, and to take whatever respite he could. But he refused to allow himself the pleasure, however fleeting it would have been. Rachel deserved more than that. Despite whatever confused link she imagined between them, she did not deserve someone like him.

He focussed instead on the rectangular shape of the box in his breast pocket, the box in which the final Blackstone Rose diamond lay. Sullivan had called him and suggested they meet for dinner again last night, as the monetary side of their transaction had been approved. For as long as Matt could remember, his father had been passionate about the recovery of the Blackstone Rose stones. Now Matt had achieved what his father had never been able to do. All his life he'd strived to prove himself worthy of Oliver Hammond, worked hard to be the son the man deserved. In this, at least, he hadn't failed.

The Auckland evening was bleak with darkness and frigid driving rain when they landed at Auckland International Airport. As they climbed into their limousine for the journey home, Matt flipped open his cell phone to call his parents.

"It's Matt. Are you two busy tonight?"

"No, we're not. Aren't you home early? I thought you were going to be gone a few more days."

Matt ignored his mother's reference to the early demise of the first break he'd had in years. "Do you mind if we swing around? I have something special to show Dad."

"Of course you can. You know you're always welcome. Are you bringing Blake and Rachel, too? Did you eat on the plane? Why don't you all stay for a light supper?"

Matt let his mother's voice wash over him in a flood of motherly concern. If he had his way he'd be leaving Rachel at her apartment, but he knew if he did, it would elicit unwanted explanation. Explanation he had no intention of making.

"That would be great, Mum. We'll see you in about forty-five minutes to an hour, depending on traffic."

He slid his cell phone back into his pocket, anticipation thrumming through his veins at the prospect of seeing his father's reaction to the diamond. Ever since the night thirty years ago when Howard Blackstone had accused his father of stealing the Blackstone Rose necklace, it had been Oliver's self-appointed mission to find it. The accusation had rankled between the brother-in-law business rivals for many years, and every so often was raked over by the press, eager to flesh out an old story for its scandal value. Now Matt had categorical proof that his father had been innocent.

"We're going to your parents'?" Rachel's voice interrupted his thoughts.

He looked across the dim interior of the car. She'd barely addressed him since he'd told her they were leaving Tahiti and frankly, that was the way he preferred it.

"Yes."

"Are you sure you want me there?"

"My mother included you in her invitation."

"Oh, okay, then."

She settled back in her seat for the rest of the journey, although Matt could sense she wanted to say more.

When they pulled up outside the single-storey unit in the luxury assisted-living complex where his parents resided, the tension inside him ratcheted up a few more notches. Since his father's stroke five years ago, little had given him pleasure. Always a hands-on man, he hated the disability that now left him paralysed down one side and unable to speak. Oliver Hammond had given so much to both his adopted sons; Matt was both humbled and deeply satisfied to be able to return a small measure of that love now.

After giving his mother a quick hug at the front door, Matt went straight to his father, who sat in the elegant sitting room in his wheelchair. He squatted down in front of Oliver Hammond.

"Dad? I have something to show you."

He reached into his pocket and drew out the velvet case, holding it on the flat of his palm.

"You know how four of the Blackstone Rose diamonds were found among Marise's things when she died?" Matt prompted.

His father nodded his head slowly, never once taking his gaze from the black velvet case.

"I have the last stone."

He put the case in his father's lap and opened it, watching his father's expression closely. He was unprepared for the raw sound that erupted from his father's throat, the sheen of tears that reflected in the older man's eyes, for the grief he read there. He'd expected jubilation, excitement, perhaps smugness, but not over-whelming sorrow.

"Dad, are you all right? This is good news. It means we have proof Blackstone lied all those years. You've been vindicated, totally and utterly. When I make a press statement to say we have located all of the major stones from the Blackstone Rose, the whole world will know the truth."

His father shook his head from side to side.

"What, Dad? You don't want me to make a state-ment? I don't understand." Matt rose to his feet, his eyes locked on his father's face. His mother's hand on his shoulder made him turn.

"Son, he is happy you brought this to show him, but it brings back old memories. Hurtful ones. Despite the fact he was the one who cut off contact with Sonya and Ursula he never stopped missing his sisters. You have no idea how he grieved when Ursula drowned. He blamed Howard for the rift that grew between the families, but he blamed himself, too. Wished he'd done more. We all wished we'd done more. It's enough for us now to know the diamonds have been recovered. Let's not turn this into another tabloid frenzy, Matt. Your father's health, and mine, couldn't stand it."

"Are you absolutely certain about that, Mum?" Matt couldn't believe he was being actively discouraged from publicly exonerating his father from a crime that many had said he was justified to commit.

"Yes, I'm certain."

"Tell me what exactly happened that night the necklace went missing." Matt looked up at his mother. "I know what the papers have said over the years, but you've never really talked about it."

Katherine sighed and looked to her husband. Oliver nodded slowly once, and reached his one good hand out to finger the stone, tears still rolling one by one down his cheeks.

"I persuaded your father we should attend Ursula's thirtieth birthday party. Oliver wasn't keen on going. There'd always been a note of competitive tension between him and Howard, which only got worse after Jeb died, but I felt it was important for Ursula that we be there. She'd been so fragile since James had been kidnapped and with Ryan being born only a year after…" Katherine's voice choked up a little. "We didn't call it postnatal depression back then. Maybe if people had been more open about things she'd still be alive today.

"Anyway, Ursula was so happy we made it over and, oh, she looked amazing that night. With the Blackstone Rose around her neck she was the epitome of Howard's success. I wondered how comfortable she was with the necklace. She kept fingering it during the course of the evening. It was quite a heavy, ostentatious thing. It must have been quite a burden around her slender neck. She kept, you know, lifting it away from her skin, playing with the clasp—adjusting it, as if it was coming undone all the time.

"As the night drew on she started to drink heavily. I was surprised to see her like that. She'd always been the perfect hostess—seeing to everyone's needs, making sure everything was just so—but that night she left everything to Sonya. When the dancing started she was near the pool, and Oliver noticed she was a bit unsteady on her feet. He went to guide her away from the edge but before he could get to her she fell in. Everyone was so shocked. No one moved at first—not even Howard. Oliver raced forward to help her from the water. He was furious with Howard for letting her get drunk in the first place and accused him of being incapable of looking after anything properly. As you can imagine, Howard was none too impressed."

Katherine reached over and took Oliver's paralysed hand in hers, stroking the mottled skin gently, her eyes distant as she recalled the events of the evening.

"Sonya and I helped Ursula upstairs, but she twisted away and shouted that she wanted to go back to the party, that Howard expected it of her. Obviously she was in no condition to do so and I have to admit we did kind of manhandle her a bit up the stairs and to her room. I imagine that must have been when the necklace fell off because later the pool was drained and checked thoroughly, as were the grounds where Ursula had been during the evening, and of course there was no sign of it.

"Once she was in her room she started to cry. It was heartbreaking. She just couldn't stop. It was as if all the stress and misery of the past two years had come to a head. She was inconsolable. Sonya and I undressed her and dried her and put her to bed. Howard came up to check on her, asking where we'd put the necklace.

Neither of us could remember when we'd last seen it on her. Of course, Howard left us straight away saying he had to find it. He wasn't terribly sympathetic to Ursula, not that it surprised me, but I had expected better of him. Eventually she fell asleep and Sonya told me she'd stay with her. I went back downstairs. That was when I heard the shouting."

"The shouting?" Matt prompted.

"It was awful. Howard and Oliver were toe to toe. I really thought they were going to come to blows. Howard had his fist knotted up in Oliver's shirt front and was accusing him of stealing the necklace. Of course your father denied it but Howard was vicious in his attack, even going so far as to accuse your father of somehow being behind James's kidnapping! I couldn't believe my ears, no one could, but Howard was like a man possessed."

"What did Dad do?" The words his father had spoken had become legend in the tabloids, but the actual facts had been muddied by various tellings over the years.

"You know your father." Katherine smiled. "Never one to back down from a challenge or to accept unjust behaviour. I can hear his words as clearly in my head now as he said them that night. He plucked Howard's hand off his shirt front and told him he'd take diamonds from him in an instant, but never a child. It was the last time Oliver spoke to Howard, ever. Of course what he'd said just made everyone think he had somehow stolen the necklace but now you've proved he didn't, and with the truth out about James, as well, hopefully we can put all this behind us."

"Put it behind us? You have to be kidding! The Blackstones will pay for what they put you through."

Rachel got up from the table where she'd been supervising Blake as he coloured in a book.

"Matt, stop it, you're upsetting your mother. Can't you see this has been difficult enough for her?"

She perched on the arm of Katherine's chair and put her arm around the older woman's shaking shoulders. Katherine gave her a watery smile of gratitude and swallowed hard before facing her youngest son.

"We've already suffered enough for the past thirty years. Your dad asked Sonya to come back home with us but she insisted Ursula needed her. She couldn't abandon her sister, not after everything she'd been through. Oliver told Sonya that when Ursula was better he wanted both of them to leave Howard, to come home. But they stayed." Katherine squeezed Oliver's hand gently, a sad smile pulling at her lips. "He felt as if they chose Howard's care and protection over his. It created a division between all of us that's never healed."

"Which is exactly why this isn't the end of things." Matt paced the width of the room, coming to a halt in front of his father. "I'm bringing them down, Dad. All of them. By the end of the month I'll hold enough shares to have controlling interest in Blackstone Diamonds. It'll be ours, just as it always should have been."

Rachel froze. A cold chill crept over her skin. Matt sounded so bitter, so driven. He'd always been focussed, even as a teenager, but this was different. This bordered on obsession. Suddenly her share broker's recent repeated e-mails made sense. For a couple of months he'd been asking her if she wanted to sell the stock she held in Blackstone Diamonds—stock which formed a large part of her investment portfolio. Obviously Matt had been working for some time to buy out other shareholders in his single-minded objective.

As much as she loved him, she had no desire to see him succeed in this venture. It was born of hatred and could only continue to fester, even if he achieved his goal. It wasn't healthy, for him or for anyone around him.

A worried frown creased Katherine's brow.

"Matt, are you sure you're doing the right thing? What about Kim? Have you discussed any of this with her?"

Matt's face hardened at his mother's words.

"I know what I'm doing is right. And as for Kimberley, she made her choice when she left us at the beginning of the year."

"That's not entirely fair, son. Her father had just died. She had to go home." Katherine's hand fluttered up around her throat.

"Home? It's where the heart is, isn't that what you always taught us? Well, her heart obviously lies in Sydney with Blackstone Diamonds because that's where she stayed." He bent down to wrap an arm around his mother's shoulders. "Mum, we've let them take enough. It's time to bring it to a halt."

Rachel's heart squeezed in sympathy as she watched the battle of emotion play across Katherine's features.

"But when will it end, Matt? When will it end?" his mother asked, the tremor in her voice betraying her anguish.

"When everything that bastard took from us is restored to Hammond hands, and not before."

"And Blake? Where does he stand in all this?" Katherine persisted.

Matt visibly stiffened. "What do you mean?"

"What the papers are saying about Howard and Marise. About Blake."

"He's my son. That's all that matters."

"Are you certain? Can you live with not knowing for sure?"

Rachel felt as though she was caught on the periphery of a Greek tragedy as she watched the scene before her unfold. Her heart ached and her eyes burned with unshed tears as she saw the fleeting shaft of pain in Matt's eyes. He held himself so rigid, as if to give voice to that pain would see him crumble.

He looked straight at the little boy at the dining table, happily absorbed in his activity and oblivious to the undercurrents swirling around them. As they watched, Blake pushed back his hair from his face, exposing the widow's peak at his forehead. The genetic hairline trait that was identical to Howard Blackstone's.

Matt's response was emphatic and final. "He's *mine*."

When they'd arrived home at the Hammond residence, Matt had told Rachel her services weren't required over the weekend. The first Monday in June being New Zealand's observance of the Queen's Birthday meant it would be a long weekend, and he told her he had no plans to go into the office and was more than capable of managing Blake on his own for the next three days. He suggested she needed the break, given all the extra days she'd worked for him lately, but Rachel was certain that Matt wanted the break from her more.

Disheartened by the realisation, she'd packed up some of her things into a weekend bag and gone back to her serviced apartment, telling herself the time off would be welcome no matter how it pulled at her heart to be away from him.

On the Saturday morning Rachel got in touch with her mother, who mentioned her sister was in better spirits but struggling with everyday things like bathing, so she'd be staying on at least until the end of the month. Taking advantage of the unexpected leisure time, she spoiled herself with long walks, soaking up the blustery wind conditions on Takapuna Beach and relishing the sight of the churning water with its garnish of white caps, catching up on her reading and watching a little television.

She was thoroughly sick of her own company by Monday night and had flicked over the television channels to watch the latest edition of a worldwide syndicated current affairs programme. She was about to flick back to the crime drama she'd been watching when a photo of a little boy made her sit up.

What the heck was a photo of Blake doing on the television?

There was one thing Matt had been vigilant about in the entire media circus that had erupted with Marise's death, and that was that Blake should never be subjected to public scrutiny. It had made the transition from car to building at his preschool an ongoing challenge. While Blake had been happy to play a game of hide and seek for a week or so earlier in the year, it had soon grown lame. It had been a complete relief to both Rachel and her charge when the interest in the circumstances around Marise's death had dwindled to the occasional tabloid speculation.

Matt would be furious that she'd somehow failed to protect Blake from being photographed. A lump formed in her throat at the thought that she'd somehow failed both of them.

She turned up the sound on the remote. All the fine hairs on the back of her neck stood at full attention as the announcer's voice introduced the next segment.

"And coming up next in tonight's show we have the amazing story of James Blackstone, better known as Jake Vance—the little boy who came back from the dead."

James Blackstone? The returned Blackstone son? But how, when the photo was so like Blake? The similarities were too obvious to be overlooked. Oh no, please no, she thought as she dropped to her knees and scrabbled around in the TV cabinet for a blank DVD to put in the recorder. It could only mean one thing, and that would destroy Matt completely.

With a shaking hand she set the recorder, then sat back to watch the segment. Twenty minutes later her head was reeling.

With her mother working for the Hammonds, as she had for so many years, Rachel had grown up knowing a little of the mystery surrounding the disappearance of

Howard and Ursula Blackstone's first-born son, even though it had happened long before she was born. When the furore had erupted last month over his return to the family fold she had paid scant attention. It was all too little too late for the mother who'd committed suicide and for the father who'd died before the truth was known.

But the story she'd just seen cast an entirely different shadow on the whole drama. One that would impact the man and the child she loved beyond all else.

On Tuesday morning the DVD burned a hole in her bag as she let herself in Matt's house. He and Blake were in the kitchen finishing breakfast, and Blake jumped down from his chair to run and give her a massive hug as she came into the room.

"Hello, handsome. Did you have a good weekend?"

"I missed you. Why didn't you come see me?" he demanded, giving her another chubby-armed squeeze for good measure.

"You were busy with your daddy. It was special time, just for the two of you. Did you have fun? Tell me what you got up to."

She let the chatter of Blake's weekend run over her like a balm. They'd been busy by the sounds of things.

Matt got up from the breakfast table and put his things in the dishwasher.

"I'm glad you're early. I need to get away early today, too."

So he was going to be all business, was he? It hurt that he could shut himself down like that. Had he even spared her a thought over the weekend? He'd certainly been on her mind.

"Before you go, I was hoping you'd have a few minutes. I have something you need to see." She took the DVD case out of her bag and showed it to him.

"It'll have to wait until tonight," he answered coldly.

Rachel put her hand on Matt's arm to stop him walking past her. Through the fine cotton of his shirt sleeve she felt the muscles of his forearm bunch into a knot, as if he couldn't bear her touch.

"Matt, people will be talking about this. I saw a television van at the front gate when I arrived today. Please, you need to see the DVD."

"What is it?" he demanded, shaking her hand off his arm and taking the disc.

"There was a feature on Jake Vance last night."

Matt snorted. "Jake Vance? James Blackstone, you mean." He shoved the disc back in her bag. "Thanks, but no thanks. I have no interest in hearing about the 'second coming' again."

"It's more than that, Matt. Look!"

Rachel grabbed the case from her bag and popped out the disc, inserting it into the DVD player attached to the small TV set fitted into the custom-built kitchen joinery.

The programme started and the screen filled with the photo that had arrested her in her tracks last night. The photo of the young boy who looked just like Blake at the same age.

"Hey, that's me." Blake's voice came from the doorway as he came back into the kitchen.

"No, honey, that's your cousin. His name is Jake."

"Jake. Blake. Jake. Blake." He started to run around the room, chanting as he went.

Matt picked him up in his arms and whispered something Rachel couldn't hear, but whatever it was, Blake fell silent and when Matt put him down again he raced away. She heard his feet hammering up the stairs.

Matt watched the DVD in absolute silence, reaching over to switch off the set when the segment reached its end.

"What are you going to do, Matt?"

"Nothing."

Rachel was incredulous. "Nothing? How can you say that?"

"It doesn't prove anything. They look alike. It happens."

"Look alike? They could've been twins. That likeness didn't happen by accident."

"So you're telling me that the media is right? That Marise was not only being unfaithful to me when she died but she was already pregnant to Howard Blackstone when she married me? You think this proves Blake isn't my son? You're overstepping the mark, Rachel. Back off."

"Surely you can see you have to find out now. The press is going to be all over you again, and all over Blake. Please, for both your sakes, find out for certain."

"Perhaps you didn't understand me last Thursday night, Rachel. Blake is *my son*. No paternity test will change that."

She wouldn't give up. She couldn't. Both of them needed the truth more than anything if Matt was to be able to continue to forge a strong bond with his boy. And, if the evidence that presented itself was true, Blake had a whole other family he deserved to be a part of. She had to push one more time.

"It might not change the legalities, Matt, but have you asked yourself why you've spent so much time away from home, away from Blake? Could it be that deep down you're afraid the rumours are true?"

Six

Anger flooded him like a tidal wave. How dare she insinuate he was deliberately staying away. Him? As an adopted child, he knew better than anyone that it made no difference who donated to your gene pool. Your father was exactly that. Yours. And you were his. As Blake was his.

But before he could unleash his fury and tell Rachel in no uncertain terms where she could stick her accusations, a pinprick of doubt stabbed at his mind. Had he subconsciously done exactly as Rachel had suggested? Was his need to be Blake's biological father stronger than he even dared admit to himself? Not for the first time he rued the estrangement between himself and his cousin Kim. This was just the type of thing they'd have been able to discuss at length in the old days, weighing the pros and cons of each scenario. True, there'd been a little distance between them when he'd married Marise—Kim had expressed surprise at the whirlwind courtship—but their working relationship had always been incredibly strong. It had been bolstered by a kinship they'd built together because they'd wanted to, not because they were related.

He reminded himself of her betrayal. Even she'd reverted to kind when the chips were down.

Was that what he was afraid of? That Blake would *want* to be a Blackstone when he grew up? No. The thought was impossible to contemplate.

"I'm late for work." He snatched up his briefcase and headed for the garage before Rachel could say another word.

Leaving later put him in the thick of rush-hour traffic, and as bad luck would have it, there was an accident on the harbour bridge. He cursed his decision to drive into work today. The ferry would've been swifter and simpler all round, but he'd planned to stay late to catch up on work he'd missed during the foray to Tahiti.

His gut clenched into a tight ball of frustration as the memory of Rachel's silky-soft skin beneath his hands flooded his senses. Tahiti—he'd been crazy to take her, but she was like a dog with a bone over the issue of Blake, and he didn't have the time or the energy to fight her. He should have. He should have put his foot down, made it clear in no uncertain terms he was the boss, she the employee. Except he'd crossed that line. Crossed it well and truly.

Goodness only knew he'd been on the verge of total loss of control at her touch. It had taken an immense strength of will to pull away and not to finish what they'd started.

And now it wasn't enough that she'd seeded herself under his skin, ensuring his nights were plagued with wanting to sink himself into her soft, warm curves again and again until he purged himself of the last hellish few months. No, now she'd insinuated her thoughts into his mind, questioning the thing that defined *him* most.

Fatherhood.

By the time he swung into the basement car parking of his building he was in a filthy mood—a state of mind not helped in the least by the brash visual reminder of the Blackstone's storefront dominating the adjacent corner to House of Hammond. Blackstone had been on his way to Auckland for the official opening when the plane carrying him and Marise had gone down. If the man had wanted to create a more dominant reminder of his unfortunate influence on the Hammonds' lives he couldn't have chosen a more obvious statement to do it with.

Well, Matt would see to it once and for all that there were no more questions. If settling Blake's paternity was what it took to rid himself of at least one persistently niggling problem then that's exactly what he'd do.

It was surprisingly easy to research paternity testing in New Zealand, and Matt was relieved to discover that, confidentiality guaranteed, he could acquire a home testing kit. After all, the last thing he wanted to do was take Blake with him to a diagnostic lab with reporters trailing behind them.

With the home testing kit he could courier the samples to the lab and for an additional fee have conclusive results within three to five days. He clicked on the order form on his computer screen requesting the kit. One way or another, he'd soon know the truth about Blake.

But one question still plucked incessantly at his mind. Even if Blake was conclusively proven to be his son, had Marise, in a final fit of defiance, been having an affair with Howard Blackstone when she died?

The next few days passed in a blur of activity at House of Hammond. The shipment of baroque black pearls had arrived, together with the first of the Pacific pearls Matt had incorporated to be set into existing designs. His hands itched to get back into his workroom so he could work up some samples, but all the while, in the back of his mind, he was waiting for that one phone call that could set his mind at rest.

On the Rachel front they seemed to be observing a truce, both of them focussing on Blake's privacy. Rachel and Blake had been virtually house bound. The preschool had warned them of a media presence every day since the documentary piece on Jake Vance had aired, and they'd all agreed it would be best if Rachel kept Blake home and out of the glare of publicity that the documentary had rekindled.

With Mrs Kincaid not returning home before the end of the month, Rachel had taken on most of her mother's duties along with the care of Blake. Much as Matt tried to ignore it, there was a certain comfort in coming home to the two of them each day—a sense of home that had been missing from the house for far too long.

Now, almost a week after sending away the test kit, Matt was impatient for the result. One way or another.

He'd decided to finish work early today and surprise Blake, who was due home from a rare play date in the next hour. If the rain that had been forecast held off, maybe he could forestall Rachel cooking dinner and suggest she go back to her apartment for the night, leaving him to take Blake to nearby Cheltenham Beach for fish and chips. Rachel was still on him about spending more time with Blake and she was right. He'd been so fixated with vengeance against the Blackstones he'd pushed aside his obligations to his son.

He'd just pulled the Mercedes into the garage at home when the breast pocket of his jacket vibrated. The caller display said "unknown number." Matt's heart leaped in his chest.

"Matt Hammond," he answered.

"Mr Hammond, it's Liz Walters from the testing lab. Could you give me your security password please?"

Matt gave her the password he'd meticulously written onto the sample submission form.

Two minutes later he snapped his phone shut, adrenaline coursing through his body together with a sense of relief so immense it brought tears to his eyes. Finally he had the proof. The confirmation that what his heart had always told him was true. He had someone of his own. Flesh of his flesh.

Blake was his son. Categorically and irrevocably his.

"Matt? Is everything all right?" Rachel stood in the doorway to the garage. "I heard your car come in but you're taking forever. Is everything okay?"

"Yes. Everything is more than okay." A wide grin split his face as he stepped towards her, grabbing her from the top of the three stairs that led down into the garage and swinging her around and around.

Her laughter bubbled in the air around them.

"Put me down," she choked. "You're making me dizzy!"

"He's mine, Rachel. He's mine. I got confirmation just now."

He slowly stopped spinning, although his head and his heart felt as though he was still on a fast-moving carousel. Every nerve in his body went on full alert as her soft curves brushed against his chest, his abdomen, as he lowered her to the ground.

"Confirmation? You mean you had the test done?"

"Yes, to both."

Rachel lifted a hand to cup his cheek, her eyes shining with unshed tears. "Oh, Matt, I know how much this means to you. This is wonderful news."

Her fingers, so small and warm, branded against his skin. Her hazel eyes sheened over, the gold glints inside her irises glowing with pleasure. Slowly he saw the light in her eyes change and deepen into something else. Something that made him lower his head, take her lips and obliterate the last remnants of doubt that had lingered in his mind.

The taste of her was intoxicating, heady. He pulled her more tightly to him, feeling her frame melt against the hard planes of his body and intensifying the swiftly building tension in his groin to new heights. Her arms slid under his suit jacket, her hands gripping at his back, clutching at his shirt as if she'd fall if she let go.

He angled his head so he could take her mouth more deeply and plunder the hot recess with his tongue. Each taste was more enthralling than the last. The texture of her lips, her tongue, gave rise to an insatiable desire that started where their skin touched and burned through him like molten metal.

He pushed one hand up under her sweatshirt and pulled her T-shirt from the waistband of her jeans, desperate to touch her skin, to feel her warmth against his skin. The clasp on her bra was an easy victim to his able fingers, and her full breasts fell free of the binding Lycra and lace. He cupped one breast with his hand; she fit perfectly, as if she'd been made for him and him alone.

His thumb abraded her nipple, feeling it tighten into a hardened peak of want. Matt shoved her clothing up, baring her breast to the cool air. Goose bumps peppered her skin but she made no protest. He bent his head to her breast, taking the questing nipple between his lips, biting gently. Her guttural moan of response sent a spear of sensation straight to his groin. He wanted her, right here, right now.

With his other hand he cupped her buttocks, pressing her mound against his increasingly hard erection. She flexed against him in a natural rhythm as old as time. He pressed her back against the side front wheel guard of the Cayenne. When he reached for her belt buckle her hands flew to help him. As soon as her zipper was undone his hand pushed aside the denim and delved into her panties, into the hot secret part of her.

She was slick with need. Need for him. He felt all-conquering. Supremely male. He pushed her jeans down farther, allowing him better access to her soft, moist folds. Her breath rushed past his throat on a heated sigh as he probed her entrance, delving first one, then two fingers inside her. Her inner muscles clenched against him, drawing him deeper.

"I want you inside me. All of you." Her voice was strained, as if the very effort of speech was too much. "Matt, please?"

He wanted it, too. Wanted it so much his head was ringing with it. Ringing? No, that was the chime on the front gate intercom. The sound was a sharp thrust of reality, forcing Matt into painful awareness of his surroundings—of the woman in his arms, of what he was doing to her, with her. Again.

If he'd stepped off an ice floe in the Antarctic and into the ocean his senses couldn't have been jolted harder.

He pulled his hand slowly from the liquid heat of her body, feeling her shudder as he did so, and helped her rearrange her clothing.

"That'll be Blake coming home." Her voice sounded thick, as if the words were sticky toffee coating her tongue.

"I'll see to him." Matt stepped back, away from her, away from the siren-like enticement of her body. "I'm sorry, Rachel. It seems I'm destined to keep making the same mistake with you. We will discuss this later."

She was refastening her belt, with some trouble as her hands shook violently. She looked up. Her lips were swollen with their kisses, her eyes still awash with the heated pulse of desire that had almost seen him take her up against the side of his dead wife's car. If anything, that was even more sobering than the chime at the gate. This was the second time in as many weeks he'd almost lost control. It wouldn't—couldn't—happen again.

Rachel stood completely still as Matt strode away to the intercom at the connecting door to the house, and after a few short words hit the button to admit the car waiting outside. She knew she should move, say something, do anything, but her limbs remained frozen at her sides, her body still racked with the aftermath of emptiness after being stoked to such heights.

She forced her legs to move, deliberately stepping one foot in front of the other as she made her way back into the house, focussing on each inhale and exhale in an attempt to force her heartbeat back into some semblance of normality. She fled upstairs to her room.

Sorry.

Mistake.

The words hurt more than his withdrawal from her two weeks ago in Tahiti. He could have said anything but that. Anything else might have given her hope that she stood a chance with him, that her love for him could finally make a difference to his life. Instead, he was sorry. Incapable of seeing that the attraction between them went beyond the incendiary physical need they incited in one another.

Rachel refastened her bra beneath her clothing, then

splashed cool water on her face. Outside she heard
Blake's ride pull up at the front portico and Blake's
shout of glee when his father opened the door to let him
inside. She knew she should go downstairs and start
dinner. But right now all she wanted to do was curl into
a ball in the darkest corner of a closet and hide.

For the briefest moment, when Matt had told her
he'd received the result of the paternity test, he'd been
the old Matt. The Matt she'd known as a teenager. The
one who laughed and loved life and took every challenge head-on and with a smile on his face. Not the
coldly driven and single-minded stranger he'd become
in the past six months.

She reached for a towel and buried her face in its
thick softness, then straightened and pulled her shoulders straight, regarding her reflection in the mirror.

Nothing visible remained of their uninhibited connection in the garage. But inside, the wounds still cut
deep. She'd lived with this for the past eleven years, she
reminded herself. It was nothing new. She'd survive.
She always had. Except this time the hurt went deeper
than before. The love she'd borne for him as an idol-
struck teenager was nothing compared to what she felt
for him now.

Back then she'd been driven by little else than hor-
mones and the firm belief that if they made love everything would be all right, that he'd acknowledge his
feelings for her and she'd be his girl. But she'd been
wrong. So very wrong. If anything it had made things
worse. And these past two encounters had only served
to drive him farther away from her.

Rachel neatly folded her towel back on the rail and left her bathroom, determined to paint an expression on her face that left him in no doubt that she was unmoved by their passion. That she could withdraw from him as effectively as he had from her.

She'd do it, even if it killed her inside.

Seven

Downstairs she followed the sounds of Matt and Blake talking, finding them both in the family room, their heads bent together over a large floor puzzle. Matt looked up as she came into the room. He'd changed into jeans and a cable-knit sweater and looked far too sexy for her shattered senses.

"I was thinking I'd take Blake to the beach for fish and chips for dinner. You can take a break and head off home now if you'd like. Have a night to yourself."

At first she was at a loss for words. She hadn't expected outright rejection of her presence, not by any means. She was on the verge of acceding to his suggestion when Blake leaned forward and whispered in Matt's ear.

"No, son. Rachel needs time alone, too." Matt's voice was firm.

Blake rocked back on his heels, a recalcitrant pout marring his features.

"I want her. I want Rachel!"

"It's okay, Blake." Rachel interrupted before a full-scale tantrum could develop. "You and Dad go and have some fun feeding the seagulls. But you'll have to hurry. There are rain squalls forecast early this evening."

Matt looked outside, a frown pulling at his face. "Looks like they're here already."

Another idea occurred to Rachel. "Have you given your parents the news yet?"

"No, I was going to call them this evening. Why?"

"Well, I can put dinner together for five as easily as three. Why don't you invite them over, make it a celebration." Be damned if she'd show him how much his rejection had stung. "Honestly, it's no problem. Blake can come and help me get things ready while you go and pick your mum and dad up. You know how your mother hates driving in this weather."

For a moment it looked as if Matt would refuse and insist she leave, as he'd suggested, but Rachel held her ground under his steely gaze.

"Fine. I'll call them now."

Rachel let go of the breath she'd held hostage in her lungs as he stalked out the room and across the hall into his study. She reached out a hand to Blake.

"C'mon, honey. Let's go and get some dinner ready for Nanna and Poppa."

* * *

Matt's parents had been ecstatic about the news. Although there'd been an awkward moment when Katherine discovered Rachel had set four dinner places in the formal dining room.

"Rachel, aren't you eating with us?" Katherine asked.

"No, thank you, Mrs Hammond. I'll have mine in the kitchen," Rachel said as she put the steaming platter of chicken and zucchini pasta on the table.

"Don't be silly, you're one of us. Isn't she, Matt?"

Matt looked up from where he was settling Blake at the table. "Mum, if Rachel's more comfortable eating in the kitchen, that's her choice."

Rachel looked at him in shock. Could he have been more blunt?

"That's just ridiculous," Katherine protested, moving over to the sideboard to collect an extra place mat and table setting. "You've gone to all this trouble to prepare a lovely meal. The least you can do is enjoy it with us."

She shot her son a look that spoke volumes and patted Rachel on the hand. "There you are, dear, now we can all celebrate as a family."

Despite the rocky start, the meal turned out to be a relaxed affair. They'd lingered at the table for a while after they'd eaten. Then Katherine suggested she bathe Blake and get him ready for bed. Rachel went through to the kitchen to make coffee and tidy up the last of the dishes. She was surprised when she saw that Katherine had followed her.

"Rachel? Can I have a word with you?" she asked.

"Of course," Rachel replied as she rinsed off a plate then stacked it in the dishwasher.

"I just wanted to say thank you."

Confusion furrowed Rachel's brow. "Thank you? Whatever for?"

"For talking Matt into getting that wretched paternity test done." Katherine put up a hand to stop Rachel's protest. "Now, now. I know exactly how intractable Matt can be, so I'm sure you had something to do with persuading him to go ahead and get the proof he…" Katherine's voice wobbled precariously close to a sob but she pulled herself together on a sharply indrawn breath and continued. "The proof he needed to move on."

"Move on?"

"To put this whole sordid business between Marise and Howard behind him. It's eating him up. I'm just grateful you helped make him see sense. You can tell it's made a difference for him already."

Rachel nodded. She had seen a difference in Matt tonight when he dealt with Blake. As much as he'd tried to deny it, the fear that Blake wasn't his biological child had influenced his behaviour towards the boy. With Blake's paternity no longer under question Rachel knew their relationship would now grow stronger.

Katherine put an over-tired and overexcited Blake to bed at nine-thirty before coming back downstairs. It was getting on for ten by the time Katherine and Oliver left, insisting they take a taxi rather than have Matt drive them home. Rachel was unloading the dishwasher before heading off to bed herself when Matt came into the kitchen.

"Did you need me for something?" she asked, then instantly wished the words unsaid.

They'd already established he needed her for nothing more than the succour of his son. But a part of her still wanted to believe in miracles—to believe that he could embrace the feelings he had for her and admit them to himself as well as to her.

"I wanted to thank you for tonight. Having Mum and Dad over was a great idea. They really enjoyed it and, as you saw, they're over the moon that the whole paternity question is resolved."

"Are you going to issue a press statement? At least to stop the media hounding you both."

"I'll speak with our PR people tomorrow and discuss the best way to handle it."

"Good idea." Rachel finished wiping down the bench top then wiped her hands dry on a towel. "Matt?"

"Yeah?"

"What made you change your mind about the test?" She hoped like crazy that he'd done it for Blake's sake. To remove all and any doubt about the boy's parentage as he was growing up and to prevent the question being raised in the media again and again.

"Several things." Matt pulled out a chair at the kitchen table and sat down, gesturing for Rachel to do the same. "It was partly to halt the speculation, but essentially I wanted to ensure that no-one else could stake a claim on him. There's no way I'll ever let anyone take him from me. I meant what I said before I got the results. Blake's mine. This means it stays that way."

"But why would anyone—?"

"Marise was divorcing me. She was suing for full custody of Blake."

Rachel sat back in her chair as if she'd been slapped. "She what? When? How did you find out?"

Matt swallowed and she watched the muscles in his throat work before he spoke again. His eyes were a flat grey, as cold and lacklustre as unpolished silver.

"I was served with papers on my way out of the mortuary where her body was held. Ironic, isn't it?" His mouth twisted in a mockery of a smile. "In death she prevented the one thing she seemed hell-bent on. Taking me for everything I hold dear."

Rachel yearned to comfort him. But she daren't reach out, not again. Instead she held in the cry of denial that Marise could've been so foolish as to throw away her marriage, let alone to believe that someone like Matt would let go of his son without a monumental battle. If there was one thing in this world he was passionate about it was family. Even his business came second to that. Or at least it had until recently.

Now it made even more sense. His bitter plan to take over Blackstone Diamonds, his refusal to accept overtures from the Blackstone family. No wonder. He had all the proof he'd needed that Marise had been having an affair with Howard Blackstone and Rachel could only imagine the depth and breadth of his anger when he'd been served the papers at such a horrific time.

"Which leads me to my next decision." He paused and levelled his gaze directly at her.

A sense of foreboding prickled down her spine.

Whatever he had to say next she was certain she wouldn't like it. Rachel lifted her chin and met his stare face on.

"And that is?"

"About what happened earlier on, and in Tahiti. It has to stop. In fact it's going to stop. There's no way I want the entanglement of another relationship, or even marriage. The situation with Marise has taught me to hold on to what I love and hold it fast. Nothing and no-one will ever jeopardise Blake's wellbeing again. Ever. And, as it seems I can't keep my hands off you, and I clearly can't offer you what you seek with me, as soon as your mother returns from Wanganui I'll start looking for your replacement and let you get back to your life as you asked."

"What do you mean, 'what *I* seek with you'?" Rachel pulled together every ounce of courage she could muster. She couldn't let him see how drastically his words had affected her if she was going to be successful in carrying off the biggest lie of her life. "We can be adult about this, surely. I certainly don't expect a relationship from you. We go back far too long for me to think that. Don't worry. I know exactly where I stand."

She pushed up from her chair and painted a smile on her face that made her cheeks ache.

"Rachel, be honest. I've abused my position as your employer, abused your trust. I don't want my actions to be misconstrued by you into thinking I want a relationship with you."

Rachel managed to force a gentle laugh from her constricted throat. "Oh, don't worry about me misconstruing your actions. You've made your position quite clear. Let's just say it was an aberration. And as for abusing my trust, it was nothing of the sort. We both have needs that temporarily overtook our reason. Let's face it, it's been a while for you, right? Me, too. Can we please just leave it at that?"

Matt watched Rachel's stiff back retreat as she walked from the room and turned for the stairs. Yeah, it had been a while. A long while. Things between him and Marise had been strained for months before she'd gone back to Australia. Marital relations were nonexistent for the better part of the year—hell, if he was honest with himself he had to admit that Marise had actively avoided sex after Blake's birth, arguing that no form of contraception was a hundred percent safe and that she didn't want another child so soon.

Despite Rachel's departing statement, there was more to it, he was certain. Just as he was certain that his behaviour with her was no aberration. He was in the company of beautiful women on a regular basis. He'd never once had the urge to take one against the side of the nearest vehicle the way he'd nearly done with Rachel.

And that urge still simmered below the surface. It was only a matter of time before they'd be hot and naked, relieving this awful pressure that had been building inside since she'd taken over as Blake's nanny—and that would be disaster, because he was certain once would never be enough.

As soon as her mother was back he'd release her, whether this thing with Blackstone Diamonds was in the bag yet or not. She could go back to her life in the UK. That way the temptation would be gone. He'd meant every word he'd said when he'd told her he wasn't in the market for a new relationship or marriage ever again. He'd allowed his instincts to overrule good sense only twice in his life, once with Rachel after her high school ball, the other time in the intoxicating whirl-wind of courtship with Marise. Both times had proven to be damnably wrong. He wasn't fool enough to go three for three.

Matt straightened up from the workbench and ex-amined, from every angle, the pearl and diamond ring his team had been working on. The platinum setting brought out the best in the colour of the large semi-hemispherical pearl.

Technically named a blue pearl, it drew from the myriad colours found in the species of abalone found in New Zealand waters, called Paua, and usually re-flected pinks through to purples and blue through to green. This particular pearl, nine millimetres in dia-meter, was predominantly green, with a hint of blue here and there. He'd drawn from a 1930s jewellery cata-logue when perfecting and personalising this design, and surrounded the pearl with twelve old-mine-cut diamonds. While the old-mine cut didn't offer the flash and fire of the more modern brilliant cut it was more in keeping with the sedate beauty of the pearl.

He nodded his satisfaction. This was perfect, exactly as he'd imagined it. It would be the crown in his col-lection of brooches, rings, pendants and earrings all modelled on designs from the 1930s. The drawings for his next range release, inspired by the earlier Victorian trends in jewellery, and which would incorporate the delicate white and pale-pink pearls he'd sourced from Japan earlier in the year, were in his office awaiting his final inspection before coming into the workroom.

He held the ring up to the light one more time, savouring the chameleon-like beauty of the pearl, the blues and greens showing a faint shimmer of gold here and there. What you initially saw was not necessarily what you got with these stunning pearls. Each one was a precious gift of colour. This one in particular was exquisite.

It reminded him of Rachel.

Hell, where had that come from?

He placed the ring in its display case and snapped it closed and wished he could turn off the thought as easily as he'd shut the lid on the box.

Rachel. She invaded his thoughts on a regular basis. Not just his thoughts, he admitted to himself. There was an ache deep inside that she'd awakened—an ache he'd suppressed since the estrangement with Marise and which he'd kept firmly tamped down in the months since her death.

Damn. It was wrong, unforgivably wrong, but he wanted Rachel with a longing he dared not give in to. No, he had to remind himself it was an abuse of trust, an abuse of her position in his home. He was a father first, head of House of Hammond second, and on the verge of having the controlling say in the company of the man who'd brought his family nothing but pain and regret. That was enough. It had to be.

Matt returned the ring to the vault, slipping it into the drawer housing each of the pieces of the collection.

He paused in his actions to savour the sense of anticipation that came with imagining the Blackstone family's collective reaction when he achieved his goal. He'd given his vow over Howard Blackstone's grave that Blackstone would regret having messed with the Hammonds. Matt's next move against them would show them all he was a force to be reckoned with. Howard Blackstone would spin in his grave if he knew that a Hammond would be pulling his company's strings very shortly.

Back in his office Matt attended to his paperwork, most urgent of which was a press release waiting for his approval. He skimmed over the details. In it his PR team issued the DNA results and thereby quelled any further speculation about Blake's paternity. They also stated that the family had no further comment and wished to continue with their lives uninterrupted. Matt scrawled his initials on the sheet in approval. He was about to fire the sheet into his out-box when he suddenly hesitated. The timing of the release could be important. To ensure it had maximum exposure, he decided to wait a few days.

He pushed his chair back from his desk and leaned back, staring at the photo on his desk. He'd become so accustomed to its presence he barely even looked at it these days. Taken early on in his marriage to Marise, it was one of those fun candid shots that take a slice out of time and preserve it forever.

They'd known she was pregnant when the picture was taken, and he'd been ecstatic about the news.

Marise had been more reserved. It had happened far sooner than she'd expected; in fact, she'd already been expecting when they'd exchanged vows in a rapidly cobbled-together wedding earlier that year. Looking back, they'd rushed everything, so they hadn't taken a moment to see the cracks that formed early on in their relationship.

Matt picked up the photo and held it in his hand, one finger tracing the outline of Marise's face. With her lush red hair pushed back off her face by the breeze, she was a picture of feminine beauty, but that old familiar pull that he'd felt when he'd first met her was gone. She'd been like a sought-after precious and rare gem and he'd had to have her. He'd believed that all he needed to complete his life was a wife and a family. Kim had urged him to be cautious when she'd heard of the romance, calling him from Auckland when news of his liaison hit the tabloids. But he'd been drunk on the power of passion and excitement, and it had clouded his judgement just as effectively as alcohol would.

He thought back to the first time he'd seen her. She was tall and slender, a lot like her sister, Briana, in build. But where Briana was blonde, Marise had red hair. A red so rich and intense it had perfectly offset her fair skin and green eyes. Everything about her had been full of energy and activity, yet underlined with an air of fragility that had appealed to his masculine instincts on every level. And then there was her charm, which had melted even the stoniest hearts.

She'd loved her job at Blackstone Diamonds' marketing division and had been intensely proud to be associated with them. He'd taken her away from all that. From everything that had given her life and vigour. He'd believed his love for her would be enough to compensate for it all. But he'd been horribly wrong.

His finger stilled as the last image he remembered of Marise poured back into his mind—of her body, cold and lifeless in the steel drawer of the mortuary. The glorious red hair lank and matted against the side of her head.

Matt slid the photo into his briefcase. He'd give it to Blake to keep in his room. Rachel had said that every night they "told" Marise what Blake had been up to that day. Perhaps the photo would help delineate the line between Rachel and his mother in the little boy's mind. Make it easier for him when Rachel left for good.

As he went to shut the case, his eyes lingered on the photo one more time. Something niggled beneath the surface of his mind. Something he just couldn't put his finger on. It wasn't until he was in the Mercedes and heading over the Auckland Harbour Bridge that the niggle developed into a full-blown realisation.

Marise had usually worn her hair in layered feathers brushed forward to frame her face, but in the photo he'd had in his office her forehead and hairline had been exposed by the wind. Although her widow's peak wasn't as prominent as Blake's it was, nevertheless, there. The documentary piece the other night had laboured the point, ad infinitum, that such a hairline was hereditary, but to Matt's knowledge, neither of Marise's parents had such a hairline, nor did Briana.

He slammed his hand on the steering wheel in disbelief that he hadn't realised the importance earlier. He had to be sure before he could make any kind of statement, but if he was right then everyone had been barking up the wrong tree all along.

Howard Blackstone had indeed fathered a child out of wedlock. But instead of it being Blake, could it have been Marise?

Eight

Matt splashed a generous measure of whiskey into the cut-crystal tumbler on his desk, then lifted the single malt to his lips.

He was right. He knew he was. Now all he had to do was prove it. His desk was scattered with photos and news clips. Pictures of Marise, of Howard, of Blake—and of Barbara and Ray Davenport, and of Briana.

It was all there in front of him. Proof.

He picked up the picture of Barbara and Ray and studied it carefully. They looked happy enough together but if his theory was correct it hadn't always been so. Barbara Davenport had been Howard's secretary thirty years ago. It was looking more and more likely that she'd been a lot more than that.

So how, then, had she managed to get hold of the Blackstone Rose necklace? Had she been at Ursula's thirtieth birthday party that night? He knew his parents had been there, but after the distress it had caused Katherine to relive the evening the other night, he knew he couldn't ask her. Maybe Briana would know. Granted, she hadn't yet been born when the necklace was stolen, but things had a way of being discussed in families that over time left dormant knowledge sitting in a child's mind.

He looked at his watch and judged the two-hour time difference between Melbourne and Auckland. It wasn't too late to call. He lifted the phone from its cradle. It'd been too long since he'd talked with his brother, Jarrod, anyway. This way he could kill two birds with one stone.

An hour later Matt reset the telephone handpiece in its stand. With what Briana had been able to tell him, he was convinced that Barbara had been pregnant by Howard. What had driven her to steal the necklace he could only speculate, but he would lay money on the fact that Howard had rejected his secretary once she'd told him she was expecting his child.

Marise's birth date was circled on the sheet of paper in front of him, together with the date of Ursula's party and the time he now knew Barbara had left her position as Howard's secretary. Given the timeline of when Temana Sullivan's father had acquired the pear-shaped stone, now safely in Danielle Hammond's creative hands, coinciding with the date the Davenport girls were enrolled for a private-school education, it all made sense.

Had Marise had some idea of the ramifications of the possession of the four round pink diamonds that she'd secreted in Briana's safe? Had she suspected, or even known, that Howard Blackstone was her real father?

All this time Matt had been plagued with the belief that he had failed Marise in some fundamental way, that the collapse of their marriage had been his fault entirely and that he'd been too focussed on business to hold on to his wife in the months before she'd left. But now he realized many of the failures in her life had occurred long before he'd come onto the scene. She'd been raised living a lie. Possibly even spurned by her real father before her birth.

Still, Marise must have convinced Howard of the truth. The vast private jewellery collection she'd been bequeathed was worth millions. A man like Blackstone didn't just give something like that away to someone as ephemeral as a mistress.

Had it been Blackstone's idea that she divorce Matt and go for full custody of Blake? Anger coiled tight and low in his belly. He'd lay odds on that being true.

He owed it to Marise to prove it. Theirs might not have been the happiest marriage on the planet but failure came on both sides of the marital bed. If he could do anything for her now, it would be to prove that Howard Blackstone was her father.

But a photo alone wasn't proof. Somehow he had to convince the Blackstone children to release their father's DNA information so it could be proven without a shadow of a doubt that Marise had been his child. With the current climate between them, and with what they had coming to them when he achieved the majority share holding he was after, he doubted they'd be forthcoming. But in all his years of business he'd learned one thing was paramount—if you waited, nothing came to you. If you wanted something, you had to reach out and take it with both hands.

"Matt? What are you doing still up?"

He wheeled around at the sound of Rachel's voice at the door. She was wrapped up in a voluminous dressing gown, her hair tousled and a pressure mark on her cheek from her pillow case. His fingers itched to reach out and touch the pink line on her face. Instead he gripped the tumbler in his hand that much tighter.

"Just expanding a theory."

Rachel moved around the desk, and he watched as her eyes scanned the pictures and papers he had spread there.

"A theory? I thought you'd sorted out the whole thing about Blake to your satisfaction. You can't go much further than the DNA result you got. What are you trying to prove now?"

Rachel reached for the picture he'd brought home from the office and he watched as her expression changed slightly, a quizzical frown appearing between her brows. Had she noticed what he had?

"I haven't seen this picture before," she said.

"I brought it home from work today. I thought Blake might like it in his room."

"That's a great idea."

The frown on her face deepened.

"I never saw her with her hair like this before. Is that a widow's peak at her hairline?"

"Yes, it is. I don't know why I didn't consider it before." Matt took the picture from Rachel and laid it back down on the table, next to the one of Howard Blackstone that he'd printed off from an archived newspaper article on the internet.

"My goodness! Am I seeing what I think I'm seeing?" Her voice was laced with incredulity.

"Tell me what you see."

If Rachel had made the same connection he had, then it lent weight to his theory.

"The hairline." She pointed with her finger to first Howard's photo, then Marise's. "The shape of their foreheads, their eyes. Granted her nose and chin are different, but anyone could be forgiven for thinking they're related."

"I think they're related, all right. I believe that Blackstone was her father."

"Her father! But how?" Rachel snapped up the pictures again and studied them more closely.

"Marise's mother, Barbara, worked as Blackstone's secretary back in the late seventies. She resigned in seventy-eight. Marise was born a few months later."

"Why would no one have noticed the resemblance before? Why now?"

Matt took a sip of his whiskey, then put the glass down; he didn't really feel like drinking anymore. Instead, his senses were being drummed into awareness by Rachel's closeness, by the warmth that radiated from her body so close to his, by the subtle scent she wore and which wove around him like a silken trap. He stepped away from the desk and sat down in his chair on the opposite side.

"No one had ever looked for it before. Barbara and Ray moved to Melbourne when she left Blackstone Diamonds. They'd been married a few years. It was only natural to assume that Marise was Ray's daughter."

"So what are you going to do now?"

"I'm going to prove that Marise wasn't having an affair with Howard Blackstone."

"Is that the only reason? To prove that she wasn't being unfaithful to you?"

"Isn't that enough? Don't you think it's better for Blake to know that his mother wasn't an unprincipled money-grabbing tramp like the media have referred to her since before the crash? One day it'll all come out again. You know it will. For all her faults, he needs to know she wasn't that kind of person."

Rachel rubbed her hand across her eyes. "Of course, that makes sense. I'm sorry. I'm tired. I should have thought of that."

"You should go back to bed. What are you doing up, anyway?" He flicked a glance at his watch. It was one o'clock in the morning. They should all be in bed.

His body tautened at the thought. In bed. Together. He resolutely shoved the thought back down into the dark place it belonged.

"I wanted to get some eucalyptus for Blake's humidifier. He sounded a bit chesty at bedtime and his coughing woke me a while ago. He settled straight down again, but I thought it would be a good idea to get the humidifier going just to make sure it doesn't get any worse."

"You head back to bed. I'll take care of it."

"It's no problem."

"You're dead on your feet. Don't worry. I'll see to him."

"Okay then." She turned to leave the room, but hesitated at the doorway. "Matt, how are you going to prove that Howard Blackstone was Marise's father? Kimberley Perrini and Ryan Blackstone aren't going to be too happy about a new skeleton in their father's closet, especially not so soon after their brother has resurfaced."

"It's not their happiness I'm concerned about. Don't worry, I'll deal with it."

Matt flexed his hands and counted the minutes to the time when Kimberley Perrini would be at her desk at Blackstone's head office and he could call and tell her what he wanted of her.

Six months ago it would have been simple. He'd have known that no matter what, he could have counted on his cousin's support. But things had changed. Drastically. So drastically they were barely even on speaking terms anymore. Her doing, his choice. By returning to Blackstone's the way she did with no notice, no warning, she'd effectively cut herself off from him and House of Hammond. It was little wonder he'd rejected her overtures after Marise had died—who wouldn't when it was Kim's own father Marise had been with. But in the light of what he now believed, he had to hope that Kim would see things his way.

He switched on his laptop and attached to an e-mail two pictures that showed the similarities between

Marise and Howard. The more often he looked at them the more he was convinced he was right.

But would Kim feel the same way? Would she want to find out that a woman she'd only tolerated for Matt's sake was in fact her half sister? He didn't doubt that Ryan would do his best to forestall any attempt to create a familial link between his father and Marise. The guy's tenacity knew no bounds, and protecting the Blackstone empire was inherent in him. If he sensed any additional threat, he'd close everything down as fast as he could.

Matt picked up his phone, punching the numbers and waiting for the burr of the call connecting through to Sydney. He momentarily rued that he'd deleted her mobile number off his phone but reminded himself they'd gone past that type of closeness. As he identified himself to the telephonist and asked to speak to Kim he wondered how long it would be before anyone else knew who was calling and to whom. No doubt Ryan or Ric Perrini's minions would spread the news with the speed of an Aussie bushfire.

"Matt, this is a surprise. How are you? And Blake, how's he keeping?"

Kim's voice sounded achingly familiar in his ear. He'd always admired Kim's directness and honesty and he missed working with her more than he'd ever admit to anyone. But underlying the warmth and familiarity in her tone, her voice held an element of caution.

"We're fine. Look, this isn't a social call."

She sighed. "No, I didn't expect it was, although I'd hoped that by now we could start to mend some fences between us. Don't you think it's time?"

He could hear the hope in her voice, the gentle plea to let go of his anger. The last words he'd exchanged with her had been bitter, laced with shock and grief, and above all, anger at what her father had wrought upon his family.

"Time? You tell me. I need to ask you something, but before I can explain why, give me your e-mail address. I need to send you a couple of attachments." As Kim gave him the details, he typed them in then hit the send button. "Let me know when you've got them."

He heard the hitch in her breathing as she opened the file.

"What do you want, Matt?"

"Have you looked at the pictures?"

"Of course I've looked at them. What are you getting at? Is this some kind of cruel taunt?"

Matt expelled a sharp breath. "Look at them again. Very carefully."

"I don't know what you expect me to see here. It would help if you told me what I'm supposed to be looking for."

He could hear the frustration in Kim's voice and felt a momentary pang for forcing her to look at the photos of her father and the woman she'd known so well. The woman who the world at large thought had been having an affair with Howard Blackstone.

"Kim, just concentrate. Try to get past the fact you knew them both and try to look at the pictures with a fresh eye. Tell me what you see," he coaxed.

"Okay, but I still don't see… Oh."

Matt gripped his phone tight as he waited for Kim to speak again. When she did, she obviously chose her words very carefully.

"The widow's peak. I never noticed Marise had one before."

"We never really notice what we're not looking for."

"Am I meant to assume you think there was a relationship between Howard and Marise that wasn't sexual?"

"Yes. I do."

"But that's ridiculous."

"Is it? Was Howard so devoted to your mother that it's outside of the realm of possibility he had an affair? We already know he wasn't a saint and your mother was withdrawn and depressed after James was taken. Howard was a virile man. As much as he supposedly loved your mother he could have had an affair, and he could have had other children. After all, no-one had trouble believing he was having an affair with my wife." Matt pressed home his point with the subtlety of a hammer on an anvil, strike after strike.

"Matt, look. I know you must still be hurting, but seriously, what are you hoping to achieve with this? It'll just start up the media merry-go-round again. Do you really want that? And how do you hope to prove your theory?"

"A DNA comparison will satisfy any question over their relationship. I want it clear that my wife wasn't having an affair with your father."

"So this is all down to your pride and this stupid feud? I don't think so, Matt."

"My pride has nothing to do with it. Would you rather continue to believe your father was having an affair with someone young enough to be his daughter when he died? Think of it from a public relations angle,

Kim. Think of the damage that has been done to Blackstone's since he died."

"Damage you've been capitalising on!" Kim interjected.

Matt rubbed his fingers across his forehead. Damn. Arguing with her wouldn't get the answer he wanted.

"Barbara Davenport was your father's secretary. She left his employ around the same time the Blackstone Rose went missing. We both know what a bastard Howard could be. If he cut Barbara off when she fell pregnant, what better revenge could she have had on him than stealing from him the one thing he prized above all else? The one thing he believed symbolised his success. Marise had four of the stones when she died. It makes sense that her mother gave them to her."

"And the fifth stone? Tracing that would be the only way to prove whether your outrageous theory holds water."

"I have the fifth stone."

"You…you what?"

Matt swiftly explained his recent trip to Tahiti and meeting Temana Sullivan.

"Trust me on this, Kim. Barbara Davenport stole the original necklace and broke it down. I don't know whether the heat around selling the largest diamond put her off selling the others or whether on its own it got her enough money to live the lifestyle we both know that her husband couldn't have provided on his income, but whichever way you look at it, she's the common denominator."

"Okay, for argument's sake, let's say she is, and that you're right. What do you want from me?"

"I need authorisation from all of you to allow me access to Howard's DNA results. I need to know, Kim, for Blake's sake. I don't want him to grow up with a mass of lies and speculation about his mother hanging over his head. You know what that's like. You don't want to put him through that, do you?"

He waited for what felt like an aeon before she replied.

"Okay, I'll do what I can to ensure Ryan and Jake give their consent."

"Thank you, Kim."

"Don't thank me yet. You might have my agreement, but Ryan and Jake are going to be a lot harder to convince. We have a meeting scheduled shortly. I'll try to call you back later today."

Nine

Matt spent the better part of the day working desperately to distract himself from the agony of waiting for Kim's call. In the end it was after five before his secretary buzzed through to say she was on the line.

"What did they say?" Matt asked as he picked up the phone.

"It wasn't easy, but I have their agreement." She sounded weary even though it was still only midafternoon in Sydney.

"Excellent. I'll get things rolling from this end." He wanted to punch the air.

"Hold up a minute. They have made some stipulations and, to be honest, we're in unanimous agreement on this."

A frisson of disquiet skittered down his spine. "Go on."

"Obviously you want some kind of public statement about the outcome of the DNA comparison if it proves your theory is correct—and I'd like to say that both Ryan and Jake are very doubtful of this."

"I had considered that a press release would be the best way of nipping this whole thing in the bud." He didn't want to tell her about his own recent fears about Blake and that he was sitting on the release of a statement that proved his fatherhood of his son. He was glad now he'd waited. Imagine the impact if both statements were released at the same time.

"We've done a little research and understand that if you can provide something of Marise's—a toothbrush, a hairbrush, even some hair that might still be on an item of clothing—the lab in Canberra that identified Howard's remains is prepared to rush through the comparison. However, the results will be returned to us. We are prepared to inform you of the outcome, of course, but even in the event you're proven correct you will have no physical proof, there will be no statement issued and no acknowledgement of the relationship, unless you agree to one thing."

"What?" Matt bit the word out through a clenched jaw. He could see where this was going and he didn't like it one little bit.

"You are to withdraw from the takeover bid, stop your buyout."

A wave of fury swelled through him. His first instinct was to growl "Never!" and slam down the phone, but he reined in his fury just that little bit and harnessed the control he needed.

"You can't be serious."

"That's our offer, take it or leave it."

"And if I leave it?"

"How can you even ask that? Maybe you should be asking yourself the real reason why you want to know about Marise and Howard. From here it sounds more like you're doing it for yourself than for Blake. When you can answer yourself honestly, call me back and let me know what you want to do." Then she hung up.

Matt was furious. With himself and with Kim. But he had to admit it, they held all the cards and they knew exactly how to deal them. Without the Blackstone children's permission he'd never get access to their father's DNA records. At a stretch he might be able to get some comparative kinship test done if he could find anything of Kim's still lying around, but he'd been ruthless in purging her workspace—and the Hammond-owned town house that had been provided as part of her employment package—when she'd told him she was staying in Australia. He'd overseen the movers as they boxed up every last item and had it shipped to her without so much as a personal note.

Given how thorough he'd been to strip every last thing of Kim's from wherever she'd left her personal stamp, Matt wasn't prepared to think about why he still hadn't let go of his dead wife's possessions.

He'd allowed himself to be manipulated into a tight corner, and there was only one way out. To agree. But agreement went against everything he'd been working so hard for. Was it enough simply to know for himself what the results were? Would that be enough for Blake in years to come?

Ever since his grandfather, Jebediah Hammond, had signed over his mining leases to Howard Blackstone, it had been his father, Oliver's, greatest goal to regain control of the diamonds that Blackstone had built his empire on. That goal had become Matt's and with the rift between the families wider than ever, he had been even more determined to see his father's dream realised.

But if Marise was truly Howard's daughter, wasn't his agenda thereby altered? Weren't the anger and the bitterness that had festered deep inside him falsely bred? His entire perception had to shift.

Matt wasn't a man accustomed to making mistakes. Every last detail had to be perfect before he would commit. Not for him the highs and lows of speculation and risk. No. He had to be certain that if he called a halt to his buy up of Blackstone Diamonds shares that it was for all the right reasons.

If he agreed to the Blackstone children's condition he was faced with the prospect of fielding his father's disappointment. While he'd been able to privately vindicate his father of the theft of the Blackstone Rose, and while the re-emergence of James Blackstone, as Jake Vance, had cleared his parents in his abduction, there still remained his father's one bug bear.

The mines.

Legend had grown around his father's final words to Howard Blackstone on the fateful night the necklace had been stolen. *"Diamonds that belong to the*

Hammonds I would take from you in a heartbeat, you bastard, but never a child."

There was no argument. A child's needs came before everything. Even a father's. And Blake deserved to grow up without the cloud of scandal over his mother's death hovering over his head. Damn. For his own peace of mind he needed to know the answer. The rest, well, he'd have to think about that.

He picked up the phone. They thought they had him, but he'd find some way out of this. A way to break beyond their conditions. Right now it was more important to get things under way. When Kim picked up at the other end he cut straight to the point.

"I'll send you what you need to get this started," he enunciated carefully, determined not to show so much as a crack in his control.

"So you've agreed? You're withdrawing from the takeover? Matt, I'm so relieved, I knew you'd—"

"No." He said the word quietly.

"No? What do you mean, no?" Kim's confusion was clear in her voice.

"Just get the tests done."

"But—"

"The tests, Kim. That's all for now." He put down the receiver. Without his agreement would they change their minds about getting the comparison done? It was a risk he was willing to take. Their consent to go ahead with the testing had been a telling moment. By now he'd lay odds they wanted answers almost as much as he did.

* * *

When he got home he was surprised to find the house in darkness. Rachel's car wasn't where it was usually parked and there was no sign of either her or Blake. It was late. A sense of alarm washed through his body. Where were they? Had something happened to them?

From the kitchen he started to dial the numbers to Rachel's mobile phone when he heard her key in the front door. He sped through to the entrance hall. She was alone. He caught her by the arm as she swung the door shut and reset the dead lock.

"Where have you been? Where's Blake?"

Rachel shook herself free. "Blake's with your mum and dad. Mrs Hammond called me to see if she could have him overnight. I didn't think you'd have a problem with that. Do you?"

He was overreacting. The by-product of too much frustration, and not all of it centred on his conversation with Kimberley Perrini.

"Of course not. Just keep me in the loop next time."

He stepped back and Rachel brushed past him, sending his body into instant full alert. He ground his teeth together silently. Yes, the frustration he suffered had a lot more to do with his son's off-limits nanny than with anything else. The faint imprint of her warmth where her hip had grazed his was like a burning brand. He wanted that brand over his entire body, skin to skin.

An aberration, she'd called their last encounter. But this sensation that held his body captive was no aberration. It was desire and need and longing all bundled into one aching mass centred deep within his body. It would be so easy to give in. To take Rachel in his arms, to taste her sweet essence and plunder her softness in the pursuit of release. If for one minute he thought that would soothe the disquieting ache within, if to take her and have done with her would bring it all to an end, he'd have followed her through to the kitchen where he could hear her preparing dinner. He'd take her by the hand and lead her to his master suite where he'd peel the winter layers of her clothing from her body, one piece at a time, until he exposed her pearly white skin. Then he'd explore every inch of her in as leisurely a fashion as he was capable of.

His hands shook. Okay, so leisurely probably wasn't in the cards. Nor was the realisation of the fantasy that plagued him night and day. Matt dragged his fractured thoughts together and locked them away in a cold, dark corner of his mind.

In the kitchen Rachel started to put together a quick meal for herself and Matt. Her mother always had a selection of pre-made dinners in the deep freeze in the utility room off the kitchen. Rachel had selected a home-made lasagne and popped it into the convection oven to warm through.

Her arm still tingled from Matt's touch when he'd grabbed her at the front door. Not in a hurtful way, but with a definite show of strength and dominance that from any other man would have made her feel vulnerable, even frightened. But she knew him so much better than that.

She hadn't planned on getting home this late; in fact she hadn't planned on leaving Blake with his grandparents. But both Katherine and Blake had been so excited at the prospect, that she hadn't seen the harm in it. At least not until she'd walked through the front door and come face-to-face with Matt.

There was a different air about him tonight. Something she couldn't quite put her finger on. Had he followed through on his plans to confirm this new link between Marise and Howard? Matt wasn't the kind of man to let something like that lie. Had he been in touch with Kimberley Perrini? Was that the reason he seemed so…on edge? She was dying to ask but knew she'd be overstepping the boundaries of their employer/employee relationship if she did so—the boundaries he was so determined to keep firmly in place.

She snatched her handbag up from the kitchen table where she'd left it and picked up her jacket. With dinner under way she'd put her things away in her room.

Upstairs, she was surprised to hear noise coming from one of the other bedrooms. She quickly put her things away, then went to investigate. To her surprise Matt was in the room, the wardrobe was pulled open and he'd taken several garments from inside and was inspecting them before laying them on the bed.

"Matt? Can I help you? What are you doing?"

"Looking for hair, Marise's hair. I need it to send to Australia."

"So you talked to Kim, then."

"Yes."

"And it went well?" she prompted.

"They've agreed to the DNA testing."

Rachel chewed her lip and watched as he moved

from the wardrobe to the dresser on the opposite side of the room. Suddenly it occurred to her that the room was full of Marise's things. Why was that, when the master suite was downstairs? Just how long had they been estranged? Her mother had hinted at trouble between the two of them, a distance and coldness that she couldn't understand in a couple that were still essentially newly wed. Away in London at the time, Rachel hadn't paid much attention to it. Matt's marital problems were the last thing she'd wanted to dwell on. Ever since her mother had told her of his sudden nuptials, Rachel had fought to lock her feelings for him out of her heart and mind.

She turned his response over in her mind. There was something he wasn't saying, she was certain.

"Just like that? They agreed? You must be quite relieved."

"It wasn't that simple." Matt stopped what he was doing and sat on the edge of the bed. "They had some conditions of their own."

"Conditions?"

"Yeah, can't say I'm surprised. They want me to withdraw from the takeover. They won't release proof of the results of the test unless I do."

"And will you?" Rachel walked over to the drawers and began refolding all the things Matt had pulled out.

"I haven't decided yet. First I have to find something of hers that can be used for the test. Without that it's all relative, anyway."

"So what sort of thing are you looking for?"

"Something on which she'd have left a trace of her

DNA. Kim said a toothbrush or hairbrush would do, but all of those things have been cleared away. There's not so much as a lipstick-stained tissue left in a handbag or a loose hair on a garment. Nothing."

Rachel closed the drawers on the dresser and systematically started to put away the gowns and suits Matt had thrown onto the bed. Everything was of the finest quality, everything typical of Marise in cut, style and colour. But not so much as a trace of fragrance lingered on her things. It was as if these were the clothes of a stranger. Someone who'd gone without leaving an imprint of their passage.

A thought suddenly struck her.

"What about her car? Did she keep a hairbrush or lipstick in the glove compartment? She always was meticulous about her appearance. She's bound to have something still in there."

"Good idea. I'll check. Leave those." He gestured at the things she hadn't yet put away. "It's time they all went."

"Would you like me to see to it?" Rachel offered.

He hesitated a moment at the open wardrobe. One hand reached out to touch the shimmering gold-coloured satin of an evening gown Rachel recognised from a society shot that had been plastered across the papers worldwide shortly after Matt and Marise had married. He fingered the fabric for a moment, then dropped it again as if its touch was like acid against his skin.

"Yes. Get rid of it all. I don't care where to. Just get it out of here."

He left the room on quick strides, and she heard him

head down the stairs. She looked around the room and wondered anew at the estrangement between him and his dead wife. When her mother had told her of their marriage, Rachel had tried to convince herself that she was happy for him that he'd found love even if it wasn't with her.

Up until that call she'd still harboured hope that one day she'd be able to win his heart. For as long as she could remember she'd loved him. First with the hero-worship adoration of a child, but then, as she'd hit her teenage years, the five-year age difference between them hadn't seemed so monumental anymore, and a new attraction had burned within her. One that had seen her take the lead the night he'd stepped in to escort her to her school ball.

She still remembered vividly how he'd looked that night. His blond hair was combed straight back off his strong forehead, making him look older, more distant than she was used to. When he'd come to her mother's apartment to pick her up she'd been breathless with excitement. Finally, she'd thought, he'd see her as he was meant to see her. Finally he would realise that she loved him and that he loved her, too.

Rachel's mouth twisted at the memory. He'd seen her, all right. He'd even allowed her to woo him, seduce him, with her newfound maturity and confidence. When he'd taken her in his arms and they'd made love in his car, she'd embraced the crossover between child and woman, welcomed the brief discomfort she'd experienced, revelled in the heights of pleasure he'd brought her. Finally she was his.

Except once the heat of their passion for each other

had ebbed, as surely as the outgoing tide on the beach where he'd parked, he'd become a stranger. He'd straightened his clothes and then hers, plucking her arms from around his neck when she'd reached for him again.

The expression on his face had said it all. He'd apologised for taking advantage of her, had said it would never happen again. Each word had been a death blow to her hopes.

When he'd agreed to accompany her to her ball she'd believed that finally he had begun to see her as the woman she'd become, but instead he'd seen her as a charity case. Someone who'd been let down by her own partner and whom he'd agreed to take so she wouldn't lose face among her peer group. He'd looked out for her like a brother. Except her feelings for him had never been sisterly. Not then and certainly not now.

Rachel sighed as she turned off the bedroom light and left the room, closing the door with a firm click behind her as she went. The last thing she needed tonight was the ghost of Marise's presence plaguing her sleep. She'd inventory the contents of the room and deal with them tomorrow while Blake was at preschool. Maybe they'd all rest a bit easier when that was finally done.

Matt met her at the bottom of the stairs, a sealed plastic bag in his hand.

"You were right. She did keep a hairbrush in the car. I'll get this away to Sydney in the morning. Thanks for the suggestion."

Rachel smiled and nodded. "Sure, no worries. Dinner should be just about ready. Where would you like to eat tonight?"

"Since Blake's not home I'll take advantage of the quiet and do some work in the library. Can you bring a tray to me there?"

Rachel nodded. So he was shutting himself away again. Suddenly she couldn't wait for her mother's return from down country and the chance to leave here again. But this time she wouldn't be in a hurry to return. There were some things a woman just couldn't keep putting herself in line for and flat-out rejection was one of them.

Ten

Matt's head spun with unanswered questions as he hung up his telephone. Kim's words still echoed in his ears. The results of the DNA testing were irrefutable.

Howard Blackstone was Marise's father.

Somehow the knowing didn't do much to ease the anger he still felt towards both his wife and his family nemesis. If Marise had believed Howard was her father before the plane crash, why had she not simply picked up a phone and told Matt? Because she'd been planning to divorce him, that's why, he reminded himself grimly. And with the full and financial support of Blackstone to do so. It was just the kind of leverage Howard would have relished.

But now he had another problem to consider. In light

of the results, Kim and her brothers had offered to see to it that Marise's remains be removed from their resting place at Waverley Cemetery and have her reburied in the Blackstone family plot at Rookwood.

His first instinct was to leave her where she was, but he knew deep inside that, with her love of pomp and circumstance, Marise would have preferred to be buried a Blackstone. His hand fisted around the pen he'd been taking notes with, snapping the tube into splinters.

A Blackstone. How bitterly ironic that he'd married one.

He dropped the fragments of his pen into the wastepaper basket and brushed off his hands. If only it was as easy to brush off the knowledge that his wife had taken that final irrevocable step to dissolve their marriage and take Blake from him.

It was time to break the news to Briana. How did one tell someone that their mother had been unfaithful to their father? That the sister they'd grown up with, loved and fought with in the way that sisters did, was only a half sister after all? He took in a deep, steadying breath. It had to be done. He picked up the phone and called Briana and Jarrod's number, expelling that breath in a rush when Briana answered on the fourth ring.

"Briana, it's Matt. I have some news about Marise that you really need to hear."

"News?" Briana sounded wary. She wasn't the only one reluctant to uncover Marise's skeletons, not after the way her discovery of the four Blackstone diamonds that Marise had secreted in her safe had almost ripped apart her relationship with Jarrod.

"Yeah, you might want to sit down. You know how I had tests done to prove Blake is my son? Well it led me to wondering about a possible link between Howard and Marise. It wasn't until I did a little more research that it became apparent that there were several links between your mother, Howard and Marise." He paused while the news sunk in. "Briana, Howard was Marise's father."

Her sharply indrawn breath resonated in his ear.

"You mean Mum had an affair with Howard Blackstone? Oh my God! No! I don't believe it. She couldn't have done something like that. She loved Dad."

"I'm sorry, Briana. I know the news is difficult to stomach." He concisely explained about the DNA matching that had been done with the hair from Marise's brush and the data used to identify Howard. "The test results are indisputable. It's possible that Blackstone turned on the charm and coerced your mother—goodness knows he knew how to do that to his advantage. And Ursula wasn't well then. Whatever their reasons, I think he rejected Barbara when she told him the news. We know she left her position suddenly. The more you look at it, the more it makes sense."

"That's true, but an affair? How on earth could they have kept that a secret, and for so long? And what makes you think he rejected her? It could have been the other way around."

"Because I believe Barbara stole the Blackstone Rose. Maybe she approached Howard for financial help with the baby, maybe she even threatened to blackmail him. Whatever, we'll never know for sure. But if I'm right, and all the evidence points that way, she must have broken down the necklace and, when the heat died down over its disappearance, sold the central diamond."

"Evidence? Have you recovered the last diamond?"

He quickly explained about the trip to Tahiti and buying the stone back from Temana Sullivan.

"Maybe selling just the one stone gave her enough that she never needed to sell the others. Or maybe she found the whole process too risky, the danger of being exposed too high, that she didn't attempt it again."

"This is all too much to take in at once. Matt, are you absolutely certain?" She sounded shaken.

"As certain as I can be. The Blackstones hold the proof that Howard and Marise are father and daughter, and they're not prepared to release that into the public domain. As to Barbara and the necklace, we know she was at Ursula's birthday party that night, and from Marise's date of birth we also know that Barbara was pregnant at the time. You know how she loved and protected you girls. She'd have fought Howard for what she believed was her daughter's right. And to avoid raising any questions, or create any disparity between you two, she'd have made sure that whatever Marise got you also received."

"Do you think Dad knew?" Briana whispered.

"I doubt it. He might have had his suspicions, but really, without the kind of proof we have today, he wouldn't have known for sure." Matt wondered briefly whether Ray Davenport might not have had some inkling about the affair, and whether that inkling had been a contributing factor to his embezzlement of Howard Blackstone's private account. But he pushed the idea from his mind. If Ray had been driven by revenge, he would never have been so adamant about returning the funds. "How's he doing?"

"He's accepted the conviction but he's not looking forward to the court sentencing date in October. All things considered, he's holding up okay."

"That's good." He hesitated a moment. "Do you want me to break the news to him about Marise and Howard?"

"No, I'll do it. It'll be a hell of a blow to him. I think it'd be better coming from me."

"There's one other thing." Matt clenched his jaw, fearful of Briana's reaction to the next bit of news. In one breath he told her about moving Marise's remains to the Blackstone plot.

Briana was silent for several moments, then she finally spoke. "It's going to raise all sorts of questions, stir up the waters all over again. As much as Marise would probably have preferred it that way, do we really want to get back on that media merry-go-round?"

"You're right. Marise would have preferred it. As I said before, there'll be no public announcement about Howard being her father." Matt hesitated a moment, anger rising to bubble just below the surface at the reminder of the Blackstones' attempt at manipulating his takeover attempt.

"I think we should accept the offer." Briana interrupted his thoughts, her voice suddenly firmer, more confident. "But, Matt, there's something else I'd like to do. As much as I disagreed with you over it, I know you had your reasons for Marise's private burial. This time I want all of us to have an opportunity to say goodbye to her properly, to remember how she was before she died. If you have no objections, I'd like to organise a memorial service to coincide with her reburial."

Matt considered her request. He'd been so full of anger back in January that he'd wanted her funeral over and done with. He was no less angry now, although it was better controlled, better directed.

A startling new thought surfaced in his mind. In itself, the memorial service would negate Kim, Ryan and Jake's withholding of the DNA results unless he withdrew from the takeover.

A grim, satisfied smile pulled at Matt's lips. He had them over a barrel. They couldn't deny or control Briana's right to say farewell to her sister with a proper funeral. He could both make it up to Briana and ensure he continued to have control over Kim and her brothers. Public announcement or not, the media would draw its own conclusions about Howard and Marise.

"Yeah, okay. Do what you need to do and let me know. Blake and I will be there."

"Thank you, Matt. You won't regret it. It'll give us all closure."

Briana's conciliatory tone washed over him in a wave of compassion. But she was wrong. Closure was still some distance away and would remain so while Howard Blackstone's influence still hung over Matt like the Damocles sword.

Matt had made an interesting discovery in the past few days. The solicitor's letter accompanying Marise's demand for the divorce and full custody of Blake had come from none other than the same firm retained almost solely by the Blackstones—giving weight to Matt's belief that Howard had been behind Marise's request to dissolve their marriage all along.

Matt would have his final revenge, one way or another.

Rachel held on tight to Blake's hand as they left the Sydney memorial service, but his lower lip started to quiver as the barrage of photographers rent the air around them with flashing bulbs of light. She scooped him up into her arms, turning his face into her shoulder. Inside she was seething that Matt could subject his son to this after all the months they'd struggled to keep Blake secure from the public eye.

She made a dash for the black stretch limousine, Matt at her side, one arm protectively around his son. Inside the warm confines of the limousine she baled Matt up with a furious glare.

"What the hell were you thinking?"

"Rachel, you overestimate my ability to control the media if you think I could prevent them finding out about Marise's memorial service." Matt sat back in his seat opposite her, his grey eyes like flint as he fielded her anger.

"You know you could have done something. Why put Blake through all this? And having your PR people make that paternity statement just yesterday was underhanded even for you."

Blake had turned in his seat next to his father and was up on his knees staring out the back window at the procession of similar black luxury vehicles behind them for the long, slow journey to the Rookwood Cemetery.

"I never did a thing to draw the media's attention to today." His mouth settled in a grim line. His expression should have served as a warning, but Rachel would not let go.

"No, you didn't. But you didn't take any steps to keep the memorial confidential, did you?"

"It would have come out anyway. No matter what Briana and I did to keep a lid on it."

"But they have every detail! From a copy of the exhumation order right down to a copy of the service. It was supposed to be a memorial for Marise. Not a three-ring circus!"

She slumped back in her seat and stared out the side window. She couldn't bear to look him in the eye anymore for fear of what she'd see there. She didn't want to find proof that Matt had orchestrated the whole thing. He hated the media but in the past six months she'd seen he wasn't above using them for his own means, and she had the deep suspicion that there was a great deal more to this whole debacle today than met the eye.

Blake had lost interest in watching the cars outside and had crawled into his father's lap. When Rachel looked at the two of them, her heart ached for the father and son. She'd worked so hard to bring them together again, and now that they were, she felt totally left out. A stranger. But that was no more than she should be, she reminded herself. There was no room for her in Matt's life—at his side, in his bed or anywhere else. No, she'd set out to make him a bigger part of Blake's life and she'd succeeded. Her time with them both was drawing to a close. After the roller coaster of emotions she'd been through so far this month she told herself it was no more than what she'd wanted all along.

As their car swept along Centenary Drive and turned onto Weeroona Road, another phalanx of reporters and photographers could be seen, grouped at the Strathfield Gates at the entrance to the cemetery grounds. Uniformed security guards at the gate endeavoured to keep the driveway clear, but little could stop the surge of activity as the funeral procession made its way through the gates. Overhead, news helicopters circled the necropolis.

Rachel gave Matt another pointed look as their car made its ponderous way through the throng and into the cemetery grounds before winding along the road that followed the serpentine canal.

"Don't worry, they're not allowed near us at the burial site." Matt's voice was clipped, and small lines of strain bracketed his lips.

Rachel felt a pang of remorse. As much as he and Marise had been estranged at the time of her death, he was faced with having to say goodbye to her all over again.

At the Blackstone family plot in the heart of one of the older sections of the cemetery, their limo slid to a halt behind the hearse that had preceded them from the memorial service in the city. A cool wind whipped around Rachel's legs as she stepped from the vehicle when the driver opened the door.

"Do you want me to take Blake?" she asked, turning to Matt as he and Blake exited the vehicle dressed in their identical charcoal-grey suits.

"No, I'll look after him. Thanks."

Briana, Jarrod and Ray Davenport, Briana's father, alighted from the car behind and walked up to them. Ray had been given dispensation by the court to leave his home state and attend Marise's service and burial. He looked tired and frail. The past six months hadn't been easy on anyone.

Briana looked upwards at the circling helicopters. "Marise would have loved this," she said, a break in her voice belying the emotion behind her statement.

Rachel watched as Jarrod put an arm around her and drew her comfortingly against his body. Such a simple gesture, but one that visibly bolstered Briana's confidence again. A shaft of envy speared through Rachel's heart as she stood slightly back and to the side of the gathering group of mourners.

Almost everyone seemed to be a part of a couple. A pale and drawn, although still classically beautiful, Kimberley on the arm of her husband, Ric. Ryan and his glowingly pregnant wife, Jessica. Jake Vance with his new fiancée, Holly McLeod. Even Sonya Hammond, Matt and Jarrod's aunt, was there with Garth Buick, Howard Blackstone's oldest friend. Despite the growing crowd, Rachel had never felt more alone in her entire life.

The funeral director gestured to the six men, Ray, Ric, Ryan, Jake, Jarrod and Garth, to step up to the hearse. Rachel swallowed the lump in her throat as the men slowly bore the coffin along the path to Marise's newly prepared final resting place.

Once again she was amazed at the power of money. How many families could have pulled this off in such a short time—being granted an exhumation, cutting through the red tape and bureaucracy and arranging a reburial in the Blackstone family plot.

While there'd been no official statement from the family, the press had buzzed for days with the news. It hadn't taken long before they'd made the connection, and the headlines had shrieked with banners such as Blackstone Love Child and Another Prodigal Blackstone. Matt had read each paper without expression, but Rachel had overhead Ryan's growled greeting to Matt as he'd arrived at the memorial service.

"Cunning, Hammond, very cunning. I should have given you more credit for finding a way past our embargo on releasing the truth. But you haven't won, not by a long shot."

Matt's response had been lost in Blake's excitement as he'd spied Kimberley and had broken free of Rachel's handclasp, shouting, "Aunty Kim, Aunty Kim!" Despite Kim's obvious joy in seeing her Godson again it was clear in her expression and that of her brothers that they were none of them impressed with the publicity that had mushroomed beyond their control.

The burial was a quiet and sombre affair. The celebrant expressed a few words before inviting the family to say their final farewells. Briana wept quietly as she stepped forward to lay a single white rose on her sister's casket. Matt held a surprisingly quiet and compliant Blake in his arms as the coffin was lowered into the ground, his face a mask of reserve.

The journey back to the Carlisle Grand hotel where Matt had arranged a small reception in his suite seemed endless. Blake peppered him with questions about his mummy, Matt answering in a low, steady voice until eventually Blake fell silent again.

Matt watched as Rachel circulated around the room, ensuring everyone had a drink and something to eat. Her warmth had lightened the atmosphere considerably compared to the tension associated with the memorial earlier. He fought to hold himself back. It would be so easy to go to Rachel's side, to accept her comfort, to gain some surcease from the deepening sense of failure that hung about his shoulders like a lead cloak.

Kim, seated on the couch with Blake, laughed and hugged his little boy with delight as they played finger games together. Blake's quietness had disappeared the moment they'd arrived back at the hotel, and he exuded energy and mischief as he bounced on the furniture. Kim exchanged a look, over Blake's head, with her husband that spoke volumes towards the closeness they'd rebuilt together.

Bitterness flooded his mouth. He and Marise had never shared such a link. Once the heated flare of their initial infatuation with each other had died down, her obsession with wanting more out of life than she had, had effectively destroyed any chance of a happier marriage together, or of providing Blake with two parents who loved him. His own failure to be the husband she needed, to be able to meet her constant demands, to shore up her frailties, struck a raw nerve. Failure, at anything, didn't fall under his umbrella. There was no way he'd risk that again. Ever. He had Blake. He had

House of Hammond and soon he'd have Blackstone Diamonds. That would be enough. It had to be.

"Matt, is everything all right?" Sonya Hammond touched him lightly on the arm. "It's been a tough day. Perhaps you'd like us all to leave."

"No, I'm fine. Don't worry."

"Well, if you're certain." Sonya sounded unsure.

"I am, absolutely." Matt hastened to reassure his aunt.

"Rachel's doing a wonderful job as hostess. You're lucky to have her." Sonya smiled. "You know, I was so incredibly happy and relieved when we heard that you'd solved the mystery around the necklace. I was wondering… Danielle mentioned that you've commissioned her to make a new necklace. Will it…will it be the same as before?"

"No, I've asked Danielle to come up with a new design. It won't resemble the old necklace in any way." He clenched his jaw. Aside from the stones there would be nothing in common with the previous necklace although he'd yet to come up with a name for the new one. It was his plan to tour the necklace together with the balance of Howard's gem and jewellery collection he'd inherited through Marise.

"You know Ursula came to hate that necklace with a passion. That night of her thirtieth birthday she'd begged Howard not to have to wear it, but he'd insisted. He loved her, in his own way, but he loved being able to show the world how successful he was, too. I often wondered whether things would've been different if my father had never assigned those exploration leases over to Howard." She sighed, a heartfelt sigh that came from deep inside. "Ah well, we can't change the past, can we?" She reached up and gave him a gentle kiss on the cheek before moving back to Garth Buick's side where he stood on the other side of the room talking with Ryan and Jessica.

Words stuck in Matt's throat. Change the past? What he wouldn't give to be able to do that. His eyes fixed on Rachel again, following the curves of her body in the long-sleeved Sherwood-green dress she wore, slipping down over her sheer black stocking-clad legs and down to her dainty feet encased in high-heeled black shoes. A far cry from the frills she'd worn to her high school dance but no less enticing. His body leaped to life; his blood thrummed in his veins and pooled in his groin.

No matter what he did, no matter what he'd been through, he still wanted her with a physical yearning that refused to be denied. What the hell was wrong with him? He'd just buried his wife for the second time, yet still he lusted for Rachel? He lifted his glass to his lips, letting the alcohol burn past his throat in one hefty swig, then turned away totally disgusted with himself. He stalked over to the wet bar where a waiter stood ready to refill the tumbler of whiskey he'd just drained.

"Matt, wait up a minute, would you?"

It was Kim, with Blake firmly and very happily holding on to her hand.

"What is it?" He wasn't in the mood to be convivial.

"Ric and I would like to take Blake for tonight." She put up one hand as he started to say no. "Now wait a minute. You look shattered. Come on, things might not be the best between us but I still know you, Matt. Today's been hell for you. Be honest with yourself. It's just one night. Besides, I've missed the little guy so much. I'll deliver him back in the morning, safe and sound. I promise."

"Rachel is more than capable of taking care of him if I should fall apart," Matt responded, his voice laced with sarcasm. But his words failed to strike at their intended target.

"Don't be silly. She's dropping in her shoes. Have you even looked at her today? Cut her some slack, Matt. Rachel's as strung out as you are."

Looked at her? He'd hardly been able to keep his eyes off his son's nanny. They darted once again to where Rachel stood to one side of the gathering, weariness visibly pulling at every delectable line of her body. Reluctantly he admitted Kim was right. Rachel looked about as shattered as he felt.

"Okay, but just tonight," he growled.

"Don't worry, I won't steal him from you," Kim promised with a sad smile. "I'll get Rachel to help me get some things together for him, then we'll be off."

By the time Ric and Kim had left with Blake, the rest of the group had begun to drift away. The brief formal handshakes he'd received from Ryan and Jake were due more to habitual manners than a genuine gesture of friendship. As he left with Holly, Jake hesitated in the entrance way to the suite.

"You know the ball's in your court. How about we meet tomorrow morning, say nine? See if we can't find a way through all of this." Jake's eyes narrowed as he waited for Matt's response.

"Fine. We'll meet. But be forewarned, I don't plan to make any changes. As you said, the ball's in my court. I prefer to keep it that way."

Eleven

Rachel went around the room checking that the hotel staff had completed their duties properly. There wasn't so much as an empty dirty glass to be seen anywhere, nor a discarded toothpick left on a table. There was nothing else she could do now but go to bed, but despite her tiredness, sleep was the last thing on her mind.

She hadn't been oblivious to Matt's distance this evening, how he'd held himself apart from everyone. She'd ached to go to him—to offer a touch, some gesture of comfort—but he'd made it quite clear that wasn't her place.

After the last of the guests had gone, he'd excused himself and gone to his bedroom. Now there wasn't even so much as a glimmer of light from under the door. She hesitated at his door on the way down the hall to her own, pressing her hand briefly on the wooden surface as if she could feel him through its solid shield.

She'd overheard his exchange with Jake Vance, and it made her chest hurt to realise that even after all the Blackstone family had done to set Marise to rest today, he was still as determined as ever to pursue his share acquisition. Her hand dropped from the door. Nothing would deter him from his path, that much was clear. There was nothing she could do to sway him back to the compassionate man she knew lingered beneath the bitterness left behind from the longstanding feud and his unhappy marriage.

She went to her own room and peeled off her dress, throwing it carelessly across a chair before padding on stocking feet to her bathroom. She took off her makeup and brushed her teeth then unpinned her hair and let it tumble down around her shoulders in a cascade of curls. She gave a half laugh at her reflection as she stood there dressed only in her black bra and panties with matching suspender belt, her sheer black stockings showing a creamy ribbon of flesh at the top of her thighs. Anyone would think she'd dressed for a lover when she'd prepared for the funeral.

And she had.

As hopeless as her love was for Matt, as angry as she was at his continual denial of their attraction, she knew she had to give their future one last chance. Before she could change her mind she dragged on a robe, exited her room and made straight for his.

Matt's room was dark; not even the spill of light

from her open door reached his. Her feet sank silently into the carpet as she crossed the room towards the bed. As her eyes adjusted to the darkness she dimly made out his naked upper torso as he sprawled across the sheets. A prickle of awareness danced across her skin as she reached out to touch him, his warmth filling the air between her hand and his shoulder like a tangible thing.

She lowered herself to the bed as her hand skimmed across his shoulder and down his bare chest.

"What the hell are you doing?" His voice was cold and angry. His hand whipped up to grab her by the wrist.

"I'm giving in, Matt. Giving in to what we both know we want."

"I don't want this," he growled and threw her hand off him and rolled away, getting up off the bed. "Get out of my room. Now."

"No." Rachel got to her feet and felt her way around the bed in the dark.

Waves of heat poured off his body as she felt, rather than saw, him in front of her. She lifted her hand again, taking his and laying it against her breast where the crossover of her robe had fallen apart.

"You want this, you want me, as much as I want you, too. Please, Matt, we need this. We *need* each other. Tonight, just for tonight." She was beyond shame anymore. If she had to beg, she would.

She waited for what felt like forever as her whispered words hung on the air. The warmth of his hand on her flesh seared her like a brand. Slowly she felt his fingers move, spreading softly over her breast and over the fabric of her demi-cup bra.

"There can't be anything between us beyond this, Rachel. I'm not in the market for a wife or a long-term lover. You're the kind of woman who wants it all, who deserves it all. I have nothing left to give."

"I know. I understand."

She reached up in the darkness and cupped her hand around the back of his head, drawing him down to her willing mouth. She felt the tiniest resistance in the corded muscles of his neck and then he succumbed and bent his head. A hot rush of blood coursed through her body as his lips met hers, as he allowed her to take the lead and probe his mouth with her tongue. A tremor ran through his body as she plunged her tongue into the hot, dark recess of his mouth and then withdrew, only to do it again.

"I want you to do this to me," she whispered against his mouth, "again and again. I want you to forget today, forget the past. Focus only on us, on now."

She slid her hand down over his shoulders, across his chest and lower, following the fine seam of muscle down his abdomen and lower still. He wore only satin boxers, and the elasticised band proved no restriction to her questing fingers. He was already aroused, his erection tenting the silken fabric. She used both hands to ease away his boxers, letting them slither down his long, powerful legs.

Gently, she pushed him back down on the bed and straddled him as she joined him there, running her fingers gently up and down his torso, lingering in the curve of his groin before tracing their way back up over his rib cage and up to the hard, pointed disks of his nipples.

His hands whipped up, lightning fast, and captured her wrists. His grasp, though not as tight as before, was no less masterful.

"Not slow, not this time," he growled as he flipped her over on the mattress, covering her body with his and burying his face at the curve of her neck where he nipped and suckled, sending a wild pulse of hunger throbbing through her body. "Not after what you've put me through these past few weeks."

He reached between them, tugging apart the robe and reaching for her panties. She was already wet with need and cried out in shock and desire as he pulled her panties away with a twist and tear of fabric. Rachel's heartbeat quickened as his hand reached between her legs to cup her. She heard his grunt of satisfaction as he felt her moisture, and she pressed against his palm, the pressure sending a tingle of electricity through her body.

"Do you have protection?" Matt rasped.

"I'm on the Pill. We're safe. I promise. No mistakes." Rachel hastened to reassure him, squirming against his hand again.

"You're wearing garters." His voice thickened as he skimmed his hands across her hips and down her upper thighs.

"Yes," she whispered in reply, reaching for him with her hands, guiding his straining erection to the heated core of her.

"I want to see you."

Rachel bit back a moan of protest at his hesitation

but took heart in the fact that in the glow of the soft light provided by the bedside lamp there could be no question of who he made love to. There would be no ghosts in this bed with them tonight.

"Beautiful." Matt's voice was strained and his hands shook as he reached for her again.

He wrapped her stocking-clad legs about his hips and positioned himself at her entrance, nudging her sensitive, slick flesh.

"Now, Matt. Please, now," she implored him.

Matt buried himself inside her with a groan, unable to resist any longer. There were no more excuses, no more regrets. Only sensation, feeling, need. Excruciating need that accelerated as she opened her body to him, welcomed him into her fiery inner heat. He strained to hold himself back, to prolong the acute pleasure of skin-to-skin contact, but instinct took over at its basest level and he surged against her, faster and deeper with each stroke. Beneath him he felt her body begin to tremble, felt her inner muscles tighten and spasm around him, drawing his climax from him in a rush of pleasure so intense and yet so harsh at the same time that he collapsed into her welcoming arms as the shudders of release racked through his body with the force of an earthquake.

Dimly he became aware of her fingers stroking gentle, lazy circles across the backs of his shoulders, down his back and to his buttocks before trailing their path back up to his shoulders again. He shifted against her and felt the answering clench of her body.

"Don't leave me yet," she said softly against his ear. "Please, not yet."

"I'm not leaving you, just making you more comfortable."

He shifted them both on the sheets, rolling slightly to one side and hitching her outer leg over his thigh, remaining joined as intimately as a man and woman can be joined.

"Are you okay?" he asked, almost afraid to look into her hazel eyes in case he saw recrimination there. He'd never taken a woman so frenetically before in his life, but suddenly all the holding back had crashed through like a floodgate being opened. And he still wanted her; although this time he would take his time.

Rachel smiled. It started with her eyes, then slowly her lips curved in a sensuous curve of satisfaction.

"Yeah, you?"

In answer Matt flexed his hips against her. An unfamiliar teasing smile pulled at his lips as he watched Rachel's eyes flare open in surprise, her pupils enlarging in response.

"So soon?" she asked. Her voice caught on a hitch in her breath and warm colour flooded her cheeks.

In answer he lowered his head and captured her lips, drinking of her generosity as he plundered the soft recesses of her mouth. He lifted himself from her body for only long enough to help her out of her robe, then he lay down on the bed, pulling her over him, tracing his hands over the soft mounds of her breasts as they remained restrained by the soft black lace of her bra. He could see the darkened points of her nipples semi-exposed at the tops of the delicate fabric.

Under his gaze Rachel reached behind her and unclasped her bra, letting the restraints fall from her and expose the lush globes of her breasts to his stare. She wriggled her arms free of the straps. As she met his gaze with heavy-lidded eyes, she ran her hands up over her rib cage and up farther to cup her breasts, rolling her nipples between thumb and forefinger, as if offering them in supplication for his pleasure. Matt's hands coasted to her waist, holding her as he lifted himself up to take first one, then the other proffered nipple, in his mouth, giving each hardened bud a tiny bite after suckling it.

Rachel was a vocal lover and her moans and cries of pleasure drove his desire for her to new heights. How far they had come from that long-ago night when he'd taken her in the back seat of his car with no more finesse than a randy buck. Five years her senior, he should have known better, should never have given in to the torment and temptation she'd so blatantly offered him during the last dance. But take her he had, and then shattered her like a fragile creature when he'd spurned her after-wards.

This time there'd be no misunderstandings. This time was only for the here and now, as she'd said, and he'd make damn sure it would supplant her earlier memories. They were both adults now, he rationalized. Adults with a magnetism between them that needed to be addressed and resolved—and resolved it would be by morning. But in the meantime, they had the night.

Rachel sensed the change in him as he played with her breasts, laving attention on each one alternately and driving her to the brink of desperation. It was as if he'd reached a point of acceptance, where he no longer had to fight whatever it was that pulled them together yet kept them apart.

She tunnelled her fingers through his hair, holding his head to her, pressing her flesh deeper into his mouth, relishing the tiny jolts of electrified pleasure that spiralled through her body as he bit gently on her sensitised skin. When he dropped back against the pillows, she arched her back and rocked her hips slowly, undulating them with a promise of greater pleasure still to come to him.

She reached down and took him in her hand. His skin was velvet heat as she slid her hand along his length to the tip, trailing over his sensitive head with a featherlight touch—allowing him close to her entrance, yet still denying entry—before sliding her hand back down again. His grey eyes grew dark, almost black, as she repeated the movement. She expected at any moment that he'd take control, but he seemed content to allow her to take her time, to relish the sensations she felt quiver through him as she maintained her slow, steady pace.

Suddenly she could take it no longer, the pleasure of prolonging the inevitable surpassed by her need to feel him inside her, to feel his possession of her body, the connection she'd never stopped craving from him since the first time they'd made love. She lifted her hips and positioned him at her entrance, a tiny groan of hunger escaping her throat as she felt him nudge her with a tiny flex.

With a slowness that almost was her complete undoing she lowered herself onto his rigid length, relishing the stretch and pull of her muscles as she took him deeper and deeper still, until she felt him press against the entrance to her womb. A shudder ran through her and she waited for it to dissipate before clenching tightly with her inner muscles, drawing him up and inwards before slowly letting him go again. She rocked her hips ever so gently, and squeezed again, repeating the action over and over until she saw a hot flush of colour spread across Matt's chest and felt his fingers clench at her waist.

She'd bear his marks with pride tomorrow. It would be all she'd have left. She knew without doubt this was their swan song. He wasn't a man who let go easily of what he wanted, and he'd made it clear that he only wanted her for tonight. If she had it in her, she'd make sure he was left with the memory of powerful lovemaking that he'd never forget, never find anything to compare it to.

Her own climax was building as she felt Matt swell inside her. She tilted her hips forward, so she could press harder onto his pubic bone and find the relief she knew lay in store for the tightly bound bundle of nerve endings at her core. And then she felt him shatter beneath her, his hips heaving upwards in an uncontrolled surge, driving her to orgasm in a splintering mass of colour, light and sensation. Deep inside she felt the heat and force of his climax as he pumped inside her, over and over until he was completely spent.

She fell down against his chest, hearing his heart hammer against hers in the same crazy tattoo. Never before had she attained such heights of pleasure with any man. She fought to hold back the burning tears that prickled behind her eyelids as she tried to accept that she had to walk away after tomorrow. Say goodbye to the man she loved beyond reason, to the hope that they could have made a new future, a new family together.

She swallowed against the sob building in her throat and buried her face instead in the strength of Matt's heaving chest. She'd get through this, somehow.

Twelve

Rachel slid slowly from the bed, determined not to disturb Matt. After their second time together they'd taken a long, lingering shower, making love in the steamy confines of the shower stall before tumbling back into the bed to sleep. How much later, Rachel wasn't sure, but he'd reached for her twice more in the night, each time subtly more intense than the last, until he'd fallen into a deep sleep.

She'd lain there for the past hour, watching him, unwilling to bring this episode to a close. Eventually reason had won out over emotion. She picked up her discarded underwear from the floor and scooped up her robe before quietly letting herself out of his room, softly closing the door and going to her own room.

There were matters she needed to attend to today. Matters that couldn't wait a moment longer. She took a brief shower before dressing quickly in her usual trousers and long-sleeved T. Their private flight home was scheduled for later in the afternoon but if she could manage it she'd be on the first available commercial flight out of Sydney. She knew she had a responsibility to Matt for Blake's care but she had no doubt that Kimberley Perrini would step into the breach and help for the short time before Matt's expected return to New Zealand.

While Rachel accepted she couldn't change Matt back to the kind of man he'd been before, maybe she could help him achieve his goal. It tore her heart apart to know that she could help him in this regard, but that by doing so would drive him away from her forever. She couldn't, wouldn't, love the man he'd become if he accepted what she was about to offer him before she left and returned to New Zealand.

She reached deep into the inside flap of her suitcase lid and drew out the envelope her share broker had forwarded her before their departure for Sydney the day before yesterday. With shaking fingers she drew out the single sheet of paper and skimmed its contents.

The share transfer form was simple enough. It was hard to believe that with nothing but her signature, and Matt's, he'd finally have what he wanted most—control of Blackstone Diamonds.

Briefly she wondered whether he'd have looked upon their relationship any differently if he'd known she held his trump card all along. She grabbed up the hotel pen from the table in her room and quickly signed the

Transferor section of the form before she could change her mind. This was what he really wanted above all else. Not her. Not ever.

A quick phone call to the airlines confirmed she could be on a flight as early as lunchtime, a good three hours prior to the private flight. As quickly as she could she jammed her things into her suitcase. She hesitated a moment as she grabbed up the underwear and stockings she'd worn yesterday, then stuffed them into the rubbish bin in her room. She could never wear that set again anyway. It was time to let everything from the past go.

A betraying click of her door heralded Matt's entrance.

"What the hell do you think you're doing?" he demanded.

Despite their torrid night he looked none the worse for wear. In fact, if the truth be told, he looked even better than before. The careworn lines about his eyes had gone; the deepening grooves that had furrowed his brow were softer now.

"I'm packing. I've arranged to go home on an earlier flight. I'm sorry that this leaves you in the lurch with Blake but I'm sure Kim will help you. It's only for a few hours. I can't stay any longer." The words gushed from her lips like river water rushing over stones.

"Is this some bid to make me beg you to stay? Because it won't work. I made it clear to you last night was one night only."

Rachel zipped up her case and lifted it off her bed and to the floor before facing him.

"Matt, I'm perfectly aware of the conditions of

our…our…" She searched for the right word but for the life of her couldn't think of anything. She waved her hand in the air between them. "Whatever. You made that patently clear to me, and if you think I regret for even one minute what we shared last night you're completely wrong. I loved every second of what we did together.

"That's the difference between us, Matt. I couldn't have made love with you last night that way if I didn't already love you so much it's killing me inside to be with you. I've always wanted you. I know you said it was just a teenage crush that first time, that girls often say they love their first. But with me it was always more than that. I've loved you for as long as I can remember and that will never stop, never go away. Why do you think I stayed away from New Zealand for so long? Why do you think I always timed my visits to Mum when you'd barely be around?"

"And you expect me to feel the same way? To declare my undying love for you because we had a night of great sex?" His voice was as hard as hailstones flung against glass.

"No, not at all. I know you're completely incapable of loving another woman again. There's only one thing that matters to you more than Blake, and even then I question which has priority in your mind anymore." She snatched up the envelope she'd folded the share transfer form into and shoved it at him. "Here. I don't want these anymore. Do what you want with them. I just hope you can live with yourself afterwards."

Rachel grabbed the handle of her suitcase and wheeled it to the door. She turned back to Matt. "You're not the man I fell in love with anymore. There's a monster inside you now. One hell-bent on destroying your own family—and whatever you think, Matt, the Blackstones *are* your family, too."

Matt watched in rigid, angry silence as she left the room, and listened as she opened the front door. The sounds of Blake and Kim at the door galvanised him into action. He shoved the envelope in his pocket and went through to the main living room.

Rachel was in the doorway, reaching down to give Blake a big hug. She lifted him into her arms and smothered him with teasing kisses, then put him back down again.

"So you're heading back to Auckland now?" he heard Kim ask.

"Yes, I have a chance to make a connecting flight to London via Los Angeles tomorrow night and there's a bit I need to clear up before then. I'd better get going. The concierge has arranged a taxi for me."

Matt's blood ran cold in his veins. She'd planned that far ahead? She was returning to the UK? Even from where Matt stood he could see the glimmer of tears in her eyes as she said goodbye to Blake and Kim. It struck at something deep inside him. She really was going through with it. It wasn't some grandstanding trick to get him to say he loved her. She was leaving. For good this time.

He swallowed against the bitter taste in his mouth. He could stop her, prevent her from leaving. All it would take was three little words. Words he'd promised himself he'd never share with another woman again. Before he had a chance to second-guess himself the door was closed.

Kim covered the short distance to where he stood.

"What have you done this time, Matt? Can't you see she loves you?" Kim asked, a worried frown creasing her forehead.

Matt snapped his gaze from the closed door and met Kim's concerned look. "How did last night go with Blake? Everything okay?"

"I take it you don't want to talk about it?"

Matt remained silent.

Kim's short laugh lacked any humour. "Fine. Yes, everything went fine last night. Blake's an angel, aren't you, honey?" She reached down to ruffle the child's dark hair and watched as Blake reached up for his father.

"Up, Daddy, up!" he demanded.

"Hey there, tiger. Did you have fun with Aunty Kim last night?"

Matt let his son's prattle wash over him as Blake enumerated his activities since he'd left the hotel suite the day before. It felt good to have his son back with him again. Right. Although it would be years before Blake made his own way in the world, Matt suddenly wanted to slow down time so he could linger over every moment with his boy. It hit him anew how aloof he'd been with Blake since Marise's death, how much he'd risked by removing himself both emotionally and physically from Blake. Sure, he'd convinced himself that he'd seen to Blake's immediate needs and requirements. What parent didn't? And in choosing Rachel to care for him over the past six months he'd ensured Blake would continue to receive the love and attention he'd deserved.

But nothing beat a parent's love for a child. Nothing else was quite the same. Rachel had at least made him see the light in that regard. She'd pushed him and pushed him until the scales had fallen from his eyes. Made him find out the truth. His pride would never have let him do so if she hadn't been so determined.

Blake started to squirm in Matt's arms, ready now to be put down. As he scampered down to his room Kim spoke again.

"You know, Matt, you never used to be this closed, this angry. I was hoping now that the business with Marise and Howard has been resolved and you have all the Blackstone Rose diamonds back together again, we could begin to take down the wall that stands between us. I miss you, Matt. I miss our friendship. Are you ready to forgive me yet for leaving you like I did in January?"

Matt thought about how holding Blake in his arms had felt. How the bond between parent and child had formed and strengthened over the years. How he'd almost destroyed it before Rachel's intervention. Suddenly he understood fully the inexorable pull that had taken Kim from his side and back into the folds of her family when Howard's plane had been reported missing.

Her estrangement from her father had been hard on her. Howard had been a difficult man to love but there was no questioning his power over his family, or his intense pride in his children.

His voice sounded raspy when he finally spoke. "It's got nothing to do with forgiveness, Kim. I behaved like a total bastard. You did the only thing you could. Family comes first. Always."

Rachel's parting words to him suddenly echoed in the back of his mind. Through Blake the Blackstones were his family, too, which put him in an untenable position if he was going to go through with his takeover. Was he prepared to risk it all for revenge?

"Thank you. You have no idea how much that means to me." Kim leaned forward and brushed his cheek with her lips. "Jake mentioned you guys have a meeting this morning. With Rachel gone, did you want me to keep an eye on Blake for you until you're all done?"

Matt took a glance at his watch. "Yes, if you don't mind. I'd better get on if I'm going to be on time."

As he went to go back to his room and grab his jacket he felt in his pocket the envelope that Rachel had given him. He pulled it out and slid open the flap. His heart shuddered in his chest as he unfolded the sheet of paper and skimmed its contents.

It was here; he had it all in his hands. Finally he had the leverage to fulfil his plans to avenge his father. His hand shook slightly as his gaze fixed on Rachel's neat signature on the Transferor line. He sank slowly onto the bed as the immensity of what she'd done bloomed in his mind.

His recent words to Kim—family comes first—tormented him. His promise to his father—the man who'd adopted him, brought him up, taught him everything he'd ever hoped to learn about the jewellery industry and more—could now be realised. Surely his vow to this man came first beyond all other commitments.

But what of Blake? What of his right to be a part of his extended family in every sense of the word? Matt would be carving an uncrossable line in the sand if he continued with his plans.

He wondered what had been going through Rachel's mind when she'd signed the transfer form, whether she'd believed in her heart that he would utilise it. He'd treated her badly this morning, spurned her love, when deep down inside he craved it beyond all else. More than revenge, more than the satisfaction of gaining control of all that Blackstone Diamonds symbolised to the Hammond family.

He wanted to be the man she'd fallen in love with again. He wanted her love and he wanted her to accept his love in return.

"Matt? Here, you can take my car if you want." Kim stood in the doorway, proferring the keys to the silver Porsche Carerra Ric had given her for her birthday. "I know she's probably not on a par with your McLaren but treat her gently, won't you?"

"Yeah, sure, thanks." Matt stood up and took the keys, letting the paper fall to the floor at his feet. "I promise I'll take good care of it."

"Here, you dropped this." Kim bent down to pick the form up, her face paling dramatically as she saw what the paper was. She pressed a hand to her stomach.

"It's not what you think," Matt hastened to assure her.

"Well, it looks like a sizable share transfer. What the heck else am I supposed to think? You say family comes first and that you've forgiven me but you're still going ahead with it, aren't you? How could you, Matt? After everything you just said?"

Matt took the sheet from her, tore it in two, then slowly crumpled the transfer form in his hand, fisting it into a ball of wadded paper before dropping it on the bed.

"No. I'm not going ahead with it. Not now. Enough's enough. I meant what I said, Kim. Family does come first. Both our families. I can see that now. And, since it's up to me, I'm going to work with Jake to find a solution to all this. It's not going to be easy but we'll get there. We have to."

He grabbed his jacket from its hanger. Jake Vance was expecting him, but he wouldn't be expecting what Matt proposed discussing. Not in a million years.

Thirteen

Rachel hung up the phone and gave her mother a wan smile. It had been a delightful surprise to find her mother back home when she'd arrived from her flight at midday. They'd spent the afternoon catching up and had shared a quiet dinner together here in the kitchen. It would be their last meal together for some time, Rachel realised with a pang. As soon as it was time for her agency to open in London she'd make her call.

"Looks like they'll be happy to have me back at the agency, Mum. They have a long-term contract waiting for me. I probably won't be able to come home again for some time."

"Are you sure you're doing the right thing, love?" her mother asked as she wiped her hands on a towel before coming over and giving her daughter a much-needed hug.

"It's the only thing I can do. I can't stay here any longer. Not feeling the way I do."

Her mother nodded sadly. "It's a crying shame. The silly man doesn't know when he's on to a good thing. Speaking of which, that sounds like them home now."

Rachel flung her mother a stricken look. "I don't want to talk to him, Mum. Can you make my apologies? I'll head back to my apartment and finish packing."

She was off and out the back door just as she heard the front door swing open and her mother's voice filter down the hall in a greeting to Matt and Blake as they came inside.

Back at her apartment the air was chilled. There was little she needed to pack. All of her clothing she'd already separated out into seasons and had packed only what she'd need when she arrived back in London's latest heat wave. Her mother would mail on to her the rest of her things over the next few weeks.

She flipped on the television set so she wouldn't feel quite so alone, although the sound would do little to ease the pain in her heart. It was the late-night news announcer's next words that made her stop halfway through making a cup of coffee and turn the sound up.

"And in breaking news, from Sydney, rumours abound of an upcoming merger between Australia's largest diamond retailer, Blackstone Diamonds and New Zealand's House of Hammond. Sources at Blackstone have reported of a meeting between the CEOs of both companies earlier today."

A merger? Rachel sat down before her shaking legs gave out on her altogether. How could the news have it so wrong? They should be reporting of the takeover, not a merger.

Her doorbell sounded, driving her back to her feet. She opened the door, still in shock at what she'd heard, but the sense of surprise swirling through her was nothing compared with the disbelief that slammed into her when she saw Matt standing on her doorstep.

"Can I come in?" Without waiting for her answer, he nudged her out of the way and closed the door behind him.

"What are you doing here, Matt? What's going on?"

He flicked a glance at the news bulletin on the TV set. "I see you've seen the news. I'd hoped I could beat them to it. But first things first," he rumbled, reaching for her.

Rachel's heart skittered in her chest as his strong arms pulled her to him. Her hands fluttered to his chest, and a question hovered on her lips but was instantly forgotten in the heat of his kiss. Matt's lips were firm and insistent as he teased and coaxed hers open, his warm hands sliding around her back and drawing her even closer to him. Tears sprang to her eyes. How dare he do this to her again. One night, he'd said, one night only, and now here he was tearing her heart apart all over again.

But try as she might, she couldn't push him away, couldn't stem the flood of desire that poured through her body and galvanised her hands into action. They stroked him through the sweater he wore, burrowed underneath it to touch the searing heat of his skin. He shuddered at her touch, then mirrored her actions, sliding his hands under her knit top, skimming her waist, her rib cage, higher.

"Where's the bedroom in this place?" he demanded, suddenly sweeping her off her feet.

He didn't wait for her answer, instead making his way down the small passageway. Every cell in Rachel's body wanted to accept his lovemaking, but every part of her brain shrieked "No!" She couldn't make love with him and survive to walk away again. It had taken every last ounce of her strength to leave him in Sydney this morning.

Matt laid her down on her bedcovers and went to lie next to her. As he reached for her, Rachel spun away and rose on shaking legs.

"No."

"Come on, Rachel. You know you want this. We both do."

"Of course I want you, Matt." She backed up until she hit the wall behind her. She put out one hand in protest as he swung his legs over the edge of the bed to sit up. "That's just the problem. I've always wanted you—and it's never been enough for you. Never been right. We had last night, and it was beautiful. But that's where it ends with us. I can't love you like that again and then leave. I'm not like that."

"Then stay."

He rose off the bed and crossed the short distance between them, planting one hand on either side of the wall behind her, effectively trapping her where she stood. The scent of his cologne wove around her, and she inhaled deeply, committing the delicious fragrance to memory. Something to take out and treasure at a later date, when she could remember this time with him without it scoring lines across her heart.

She shook her head. "I can't."

"Stay. Please," he growled, and lifted one hand from the wall to cup her chin and force her to look up into his clear grey gaze.

"Don't you understand anything I've said to you? I can't stay with you, Matt. You don't need me anymore. Blake is happy now since you've started to spend more time with him again. The night he spent with Kim in Sydney is proof positive of that. No. I've done all I can."

"And me, Rachel? How about me?"

"You know you don't need me. You've said as much all along. I'm not such a sucker for punishment that I'm prepared to be available for you whenever you want me and be shoved aside when you've had enough."

"And if I said I needed you?"

When she went to shake her head, he held her face between both his palms.

"I mean it, Rachel. I need you. I'm begging you to stay. I love you. Curse me for all kinds of fool for denying it for so long if you like, but don't deny me this. I can't imagine a future without you beside me, sharing my life, my heart, my bed." He bent his head and kissed her softly, sweetly, on lips parted with shock at his words.

"No, I can't," she whispered against his lips. "Not when you're so hell-bent on destruction. Not when you harbour so much anger. It'd destroy us both in the end."

"It's all right now. I changed my mind."

Rachel pushed him away from her. "What? Just like that? After all this time?"

"I finally listened to you. You were right. The Blackstones are my family as much as they are Blake's. It was time for the hatred and feuding to end. Conquering Blackstone Diamonds meant nothing to me anymore once I realised how truthful your words were. When I looked at myself I didn't like the man I'd become any more than you did. I don't want to be that person anymore. I want to be the man you fell in love with. I want you to let me love you the way you deserve to be loved, by a man who deserves to love you."

Rachel sank down onto the bed. Words failed her. Matt sat beside her, taking her hand and lifting it to his lips before pressing it over his heart.

"I've fought my feelings for you for far too long. That night when we first made love, I knew I should have held back. Hell, you were only seventeen. But I wanted you so very much. I thought one taste would be enough, but afterwards, when you thought we could continue with a relationship, all I could think of was how I'd shamed you and my family. I'd betrayed a trust that both our families had in me when I escorted you to the dance that night. I'd betrayed your innocence."

Beneath her fingers Rachel felt the steady beat of Matt's heart.

"Matt, I wanted you to take me. I wanted to be your girlfriend and more."

"But I couldn't give that to you. Not then. Not when

you still had your whole life ahead of you. You hadn't been to university, travelled, done any of the things you'd always talked about. If you'd stayed you would have come to resent me in the end. And I would've resented you, too. I had big dreams for my future, and they didn't involve a steady girlfriend at the time. I know it sounds selfish but you have to understand where I'm coming from. Mum and Dad never hid the truth about my birth parents from me. My birth mother was only seventeen when she had me, my birth father a few years older. I couldn't bear it if we'd allowed history to repeat itself."

"But, Matt, even if we'd had a baby we'd have had the support of our parents," Rachel protested.

"You don't understand. I couldn't do that to Katherine and Oliver. Not after all they'd been through. Not after all the support and love they'd given me all my life. I just didn't have room in my life to be the person you needed then. We were on different paths. Mine was to support my father in his endeavour to keep House of Hammond strong and growing and to take back what he'd always felt had been taken from him by Howard Blackstone. You deserved better than that."

"And what happened to that path, Matt? What are you doing with Blackstone now?"

Matt smiled, a genuine smile that lifted the intensity from his eyes and lightened his face. "We're doing what we should have done years ago. We're merging the companies together. It won't happen overnight, obviously. It'll take years of planning and hard work, but it'll be good work and it'll mean that the old hatred can die a natural death, leaving the way clear for Blake and the rest of his generation to keep the peace between us."

"Are you sure that's what you really want?" Rachel couldn't believe her ears—couldn't believe that after decades of anger and accusations between the families it was all coming to an end. A happy end.

"I'm certain. It's time to look forward, to put the past in the past where it belongs. People make mistakes, horrible mistakes, and I'm not immune from that. But you've shown me that nothing built in anger can survive. It takes genuine love and commitment to make things last. The kind of love and commitment you've offered me and that I was too stupid to accept." He cupped the back of her head, tilting her head so she faced him eye to eye. "I want to accept that now, Rachel. I want to accept everything you've so generously and selflessly given me. And I want to give it back to you in return.

"I let the failure of my marriage smother my true feelings towards you. I let it make me believe that I couldn't succeed in the kind of relationship you deserve. But I was wrong. My marriage failed for myriad reasons but I know I will never fail you, if you'll only give me a chance to show you how much I love you. I need you to keep me human, to remind me daily of what's important in my life. You, Blake, my family—*all* my family.

"Will you marry me, Rachel Kincaid? Do me the utmost honour of being my wife?"

Tears streaked down Rachel's cheeks. She could barely draw breath, her heart had swollen so huge in her chest as she finally heard the words she'd always waited to hear.

"I love you with everything there is inside me, Matt. Of course I'll marry you. You're all I've ever wanted or ever will want."

She reached up to kiss him, to show him in every possible way how much his words meant to her and how heartfelt were her own.

When Matt broke the kiss, he put his hands on her shoulders, pushing her back gently. "Will you wear this?"

He reached inside his jeans pocket and drew out a platinum-set pearl and diamond ring. The pearl and pink diamond were of equal size, set side by side with a semicircle of four smaller pink diamonds on each side to ring the two together. Rachel gasped as she held out her hand for him to put it on her ring finger.

"It's a *toi et moi* ring. You—" he pointed to the iridescent pink pearl "—and me." He lightly touched the pink diamond. "Your gentleness and beauty to balance and soften the hardness of my heart. If you don't like it I'll make you something else."

"No, it's perfect. I love it, Matt. I love you."

Their clothes disappeared as they sought each other to affirm their love. When finally, on a joyful sigh, their bodies cleaved together again, it was with a sense of rightness and purpose that overrode past sorrows and disappointments, replacing them with a hope for the future that was as strong and bright as the many facets of a brilliant-cut diamond reflecting the light of a new dawn.

Epilogue

"You look beautiful, Rachel." Kim's smile belied the tears in her voice.

"Absolutely stunning," agreed Danielle, who together with Kim had helped Rachel prepare for the wedding.

Rachel stood in front of the cheval mirror, her eyes sparkling in disbelief at the reflection that faced her. She *felt* beautiful in the strapless sweetheart-neckline gown that hugged her torso before cascading to the floor in a cloud of tulle and organza. She hadn't wanted traditional white, instead opting for a fabric that shimmered with the faintest shade of pink through the layers, much like the pearl in the ring Matt had put on her finger only two weeks ago.

Two weeks. She had to pinch herself to even believe

it was true. She felt like Cinderella about to go to the ball to meet her fairy-tale prince—except today was real. So very real.

She smiled at Kim's reflection as Kim adjusted the short veil pinned to her hair with clasps decorated with pink diamonds—Kim and Ric's wedding gift to her.

Kim gave her a quick hug. "I'm glad he finally saw sense and didn't let you go."

"I know. I'm so lucky," Rachel replied, her throat constricting on the words as she remembered how close she was to leaving Matt for good.

"*You're* lucky? More like the other way around." Kim laughed softly. "But either way, I couldn't be happier. He's the old Matt again. It's great to have him back."

A knock at the door made the women turn. Butterflies did double loops in Rachel's stomach. Was it already time?

Matt stepped into the room, tall and debonair in a charcoal-grey morning suit.

"Matt! You can't come in now. It's bad luck to see the bride!" Kim exclaimed and tried her best to push him out the door again.

"We've finished our run of bad luck. Trust me. Besides, I wanted to be the one to ask Rachel to wear this." He revealed a large white velvet case. He cupped the base with one hand and opened it towards Rachel with the other. Kim and Rachel gasped in unison as he revealed an exquisitely crafted necklace on a cushion of white velvet.

"Oh my, that's the most stunning piece I've ever seen

in my life. I recognise your work," Kim said as she turned to Danielle with a bittersweet smile. "You've outdone yourself with this. And I recognize the stones. My mum would've approved if she could see it today."

Rachel knew for certain then that the five pink diamonds had once been part of the legendary Blackstone Rose.

Danielle looped one arm around Kim's waist and gave her a quick hug as Kim dabbed at the moisture that had suddenly sprung to her eyes.

Rachel cast a worried look in Kim's direction. "Kim, I don't want to wear it if it'll upset you or your family."

"No, it's time the old ghosts were all laid to rest," Kim hastened to reassure her. "And this is the perfect way to do it. Put it on her, Matt."

He looked to Rachel for confirmation. "If you're sure?"

Rachel nodded, her heart swelling with pride that this man was about to become her husband.

As Matt lifted the necklace from its case he said, "I've renamed it the Bridal Rose. I'd like to think all future Hammond and Blackstone brides will be able to wear it as a symbol of the new unity between our families." Then, lifting Rachel's veil slightly to one side, he looped it around her neck. "We can't forget the past or remake it. We can't bring back the loved ones we've lost. But we can make sure our families have a strong and happy future together."

The stones settled against Rachel's skin with a flash of rose-tinted fire, and the three women gazed upon her reflection in brief silence. While the chain looked fragile, on closer inspection Rachel could see the links were doubled, each one woven into the other, giving a softly rounded foxtail effect that belied the delicate appearance of the necklace. But the chain was nothing compared to the five priceless pink diamonds graduated to drop in a 'V' featuring, at the apex, the teardrop-shaped stone Matt had recovered in Tahiti.

"It's perfect," Rachel whispered. "Matt, thank you."

His eyes met hers in the mirror. "Yes, perfect. I love you, Rachel. Don't keep me waiting, okay?" He lifted her hand to press a kiss quickly to her knuckles, then left the room.

"Did he say all Hammond and Blackstone brides?" Kim said with a twinkle in her eye.

"Yes, he did," said Danielle. "I know it was his original intention to tour the necklace with the rest of Howard's collection but I have to say I like this idea better. It ties it all off so perfectly, letting go of the old and moving on with the new. The feud affected us all. I'm so glad it's in the past."

"I agree. And I look forward to the day when my daughter can wear the necklace, too," Kim said quietly.

"Kim!" Rachel exclaimed on an excited gasp. "Your daughter? You mean—"

"Wow! That was quick." Danielle laughed.

"Yes, and very unexpected." Kim laughed as Rachel and Danielle crowded around her. "Ric and I are having a daughter, our own little miracle. We've hardly got used to the reality yet ourselves, but we're incredibly happy."

"I can't believe it. You barely even show!" Rachel put

her hand to Kim's softly rounded belly. That explained the wonderful glow of happiness she'd noticed in Matt's cousin. "I'm so happy for you both. That's just the best news. Oh, heck, I'm going to have to redo my makeup if we keep this up!"

Kim's news was truly wonderful. Evidence that miracles did happen—like the miracle of Matt's love for her. She reached for a tissue to dab at her eyes.

"Oh, no you don't! We haven't got time. You heard the man." Danielle chuckled and handed Rachel the posy of pink rosebuds she'd chosen as her bridal bouquet. "Let's not keep him waiting."

The three women made their way downstairs, pausing at the entrance to the ballroom where the rest of the family was assembled awaiting Rachel's arrival. Rachel's father, on shore leave, stepped forward, looking strong and handsome in his naval dress uniform. Kim gave Rachel's veil and dress a final primp and gave a tiny nod when she was finally satisfied everything was just right.

"Remember, give us a couple of minutes, and don't run down the aisle. He's waited this long, he can wait a few seconds longer."

As Rachel stood in the passageway, her hand on her father's forearm, she suddenly felt an overwhelming sense of calm descend over her. All the nerves, all the butterflies she'd been beset with since she'd woken this morning, disappeared. Only a few metres away, the man she loved with every beat of her heart waited to pledge his love to her. The moment couldn't have felt more right.

"Ready, honey?" her father asked, his weathered face wreathed in a happy smile.

"Absolutely," she replied, reaching up to give her father a quick kiss on the cheek.

"I now present to you, Mr and Mrs Matt Hammond!" The celebrant's voice rang out across the ballroom.

"*My* mummy!" Blake shouted as he squirmed to get down from Katherine's lap and raced towards the couple standing at the altar.

Matt scooped him up in his arms, holding him out so he could give Rachel a kiss. "Yes, son. Your mummy, just like you said." His eyes met Rachel's and he knew his life couldn't be more complete than it was at this very moment.

He looked around the room at the small but close-knit gathering of family members who'd made it at such short notice to their wedding. His mother and father were seated with Sonya, and for the first time in Matt's memory a sense of peace and calm was evident on his father's features. Garth Buick stood a little to one side, but there was no denying the adoration on the man's face as he watched Sonya renew her family ties with her estranged brother.

"Congratulations, Matt." Jarrod and Briana stepped forward from the group of witnesses to their exchange of vows. Jarrod bent to give Rachel a quick kiss on the cheek. "Welcome to the family, Rachel." He winked at his brother. "Can't stop her tagging along now."

Matt looped his other arm around Rachel's waist. "And I wouldn't want to," he said emphatically.

Jake and Holly joined them, also expressing their

good wishes, shortly followed by Kim and Ric and Danielle and Quinn.

It was during the speeches that Jake's cell phone began buzzing rather obviously in his breast pocket. Holly gave him a strong nudge and an admonition to turn it off, but, unperturbed, Jake flipped the phone open, his voice a low rumble until he snapped it shut again.

In the next break in proceedings he stood and clasped his champagne glass in one hand. "I'd like to announce a double celebration. Would everyone charge their glasses, please."

Catering staff hastened around the tables ensuring that everyone had their glasses topped up. Satisfied everyone was ready, Jake cleared his throat, raising his glass in the air.

"I'd like to announce the safe arrival of Ryan and Jessica's twins, a boy and a girl. Mother and babies are doing well. Father is a complete wreck!"

Laughter resounded in the room as everyone toasted the new babies.

As the afternoon progressed into evening and the ballroom was cleared for dancing, Matt took Rachel into his arms in step to the waltz being played by the string quartet in the corner of the room.

"Happy, Mrs Hammond?" He bent down and nuzzled behind her ear.

"Ecstatic, Mr Hammond, and you?"

He felt her pulse step up a beat under the pressure of his lips, and acknowledged the answering surge in his blood. "I can't wait until they're all gone and I can have you to myself again. The past two weeks have been torture."

A happy laugh bubbled from Rachel's throat, and he swung her around in time to the music. "Hey, it was your idea to wait," she reminded him. "Just think how good it's going to be. Tonight and every night for the rest of our lives."

The rest of their lives. The overwhelming sense of happiness that emanated from deep inside him settled like a mantle across his shoulders. As they spun around the room once more he realised anew how close he'd come to losing it all—and how lucky he was to have the woman in his arms.

* * * * *

Thanks for joining us for
DIAMONDS DOWN UNDER!
We hope you enjoyed these fabulous six books.
Please watch for Desire's next continuity,
PARK AVENUE SCANDALS,
starting this July.
And be sure to watch for Yvonne Lindsay's
next Desire,
CLAIMING HIS RUNAWAY BRIDE,
this August.

BRIANNA stretched out beside Ewan, languid as a cat, and promptly fell asleep. Midday sunshine streamed into the chamber, bathing her lovely, long-limbed body in golden light, the sea-scented breeze wafting inside to dry the damp red-gold tendrils curling about her flushed face. Propping himself up on one elbow, Ewan slid his gaze over her. She looked beautiful and whole, satisfied and sated, and altogether happier than he had so far seen her. A slight smile curved her beautiful lips as though she must be in the midst of a lovely dream. She'd molded her lush, lovely body to his and laid her head in the curve of his shoulder and settled in to sleep beside him. For the longest while he lay there turned toward her, content to watch her sleep, at near perfect peace.

Not wholly perfect, for she had yet to answer his marriage proposal. Still, she wanted to make a baby with him, and Ewan no longer viewed her plan as the travesty he once had. He wanted children—sons to carry on after him, though a bonny little daughter with flame-colored hair would be nice, too. But he also wanted more than to simply plant his seed and be on his way. He wanted to lie beside Brianna night upon night as she increased, rub soothing unguents into the swell of her belly, knead the ache from her back and make slow, gentle love to her. He wanted to hold his newly born child in his arms and look down into Brianna's tired but radiant face and blot the perspiration from her brow and be a husband to her in every way.

He gave her a gentle nudge. "Brie?"

"Hmmm?"

She rolled onto her side and he captured her against his chest. One arm wrapped about her waist, he bent to her ear and asked, "Do you think we might have just made a baby?"

Her eyes remained closed, but he felt her tense against him. "I don't know. We'll have to wait and see."

He stroked his hand over the flat plane of her belly. "You're so small and tight it's hard to imagine you increasing."

"All women increase no matter how large or small they start out. I may not grow big as a croft, but I'll be big enough, though I have hopes I may not waddle like a duck, at least not too badly."

The reference to his fair-day teasing was not lost on him. He grinned. "Brianna MacLeod grown so large she must sit still for once in her life. I'll need the proof of my own eyes to believe it."

Despite their banter, he felt his spirits dip. Assuming they were so blessed, he wouldn't have the chance to see her thus. By then he would be long gone, restored to his clan according to the sad bargain they'd struck. He opened his mouth to ask her to marry him again and then clamped it closed, not wanting to spoil the moment, but the unspoken words weighed like a millstone on his heart.

The damnable bargain they'd struck was proving to be a devil's pact indeed.

* * * * *

*Will these two star-crossed lovers find
their sexily-ever-after?
Find out in BOUND TO PLEASE by Hope Tarr,
available in July wherever Harlequin® Blaze™
books are sold.*